FROM THE
NANCY DREW FILES

THE CASE: Nancy investigates the attempted murder of a rock musician at Pineapple Grove, an exclusive Caribbean resort.

CONTACT: Bass player Ricky Angeles has the most to hide—and the most to lose.

SUSPECTS: Courtney Brooks—*the former singer for Woody and the Hot Rods has had a falling out with the group, and now she has a score to settle.*

Steve Gibbs—*the owner of Pineapple Grove has been seen arguing heatedly with Ricky over the terms of a mysterious deal.*

Daniel and Vincent—*the two Pineapple Grove guides imply that if Nancy keeps looking for trouble, they might just help her find it.*

COMPLICATIONS: Nancy has twice saved Ricky's life—but he refuses to talk to her or reveal who might want him dead.

Books in The Nancy Drew Files ® Series

Available from ARCHWAY Paperbacks

THE
NANCY DREW
FILES™

Case 58
HOT PURSUIT

CAROLYN KEENE

AN ARCHWAY PAPERBACK
Published by POCKET BOOKS
New York   London   Toronto   Sydney   Tokyo   Singapore

AN ARCHWAY PAPERBACK *Original*

An Archway Paperback published by
POCKET BOOKS, a division of Simon & Schuster
1230 Avenue of the Americas, New York, NY 10020

Copyright © 1991 by Simon & Schuster
Produced by Mega-Books of New York, Inc.

ISBN: 0-671-70035-9

First Archway Paperback printing April 1991

10 9 8 7 6 5 4 3 2 1

NANCY DREW, AN ARCHWAY PAPERBACK and colophon are registered trademarks of Simon & Schuster.

THE NANCY DREW FILES is a trademark of Simon & Schuster.

Cover art by Tom Galasinski

Printed in the U.S.A.

IL 6 +

HOT PURSUIT

Chapter

One

DO YOU THINK Woody and the Hot Rods will be on that seaplane?" asked Bess Marvin, pointing to the small silver spot on the horizon.

"I may be a detective, but I haven't mastered the fine art of seeing into the future—or into a plane yet," said Nancy Drew, laughing gently at her friend. She brushed her reddish blond hair off her face and reached for her sunglasses. The rays of the warm Caribbean sun danced on the water like sparkling diamonds, making it hard for her to even see the plane.

Bess's cousin George Fayne jogged up to the girls just then. Her short, dark hair was slicked back from her face, and her skin glistened with drops of water. "The water's great!" she said, grabbing a towel and drying off.

1

The three friends were vacationing at Pineapple Grove, a resort on the Caribbean island of St. John. From their position under a cluster of coconut palms, they could keep an eye on the other end of the cove, where seaplanes and water taxis landed to drop off and pick up resort guests.

Bess was perched on the edge of her lounge chair now, her hands cupped above her pale blue eyes, shading them as she stared at the small plane that was now taxiing through the surf. "I'll just die if we don't get a chance to meet the guys in the band."

"Admit it, Bess," George said, reaching for her suntan lotion. "When it comes to guys, you'd like to meet them all—rock stars or not!"

Bess stopped staring at the seaplane long enough to give her cousin a look of mock indignation. "You just don't appreciate how lucky we are to be here at the same time the band's going to be filming a video."

Bess closed her eyes just then and crooned softly, " 'Look at the sky above—and launch into love—' "

"Oh no," George groaned, rolling her eyes. "Not another Hot Rods medley by Bess Marvin!" She finished applying sun lotion and stretched her long, athletic figure out on a lounge chair, closing her eyes. "Don't wake me up until it's over."

Nancy glanced at her two friends, smiling to herself. Sometimes it was hard to believe Bess and George were cousins. Curvy, blond Bess's main preoccupation was with guys, and her taller, athletic cousin was preoccupied with sports—and guys, sometimes.

Bess stopped singing. "Okay, okay. The Hot Rods may be a little better than I am," she admitted. "Do you think they're on that plane?" she said, staring across the cove again.

"Maybe. They could be traveling in disguise to avoid screaming fans," George teased.

"I'd recognize them anywhere," Bess went on, as if she were the public relations agent for the group. "Dark-haired, exotic Enrique 'Ricky' Angeles, wacky redheaded Woody Neal, and the gorgeous, blond Tucker Dawson. He's my absolute favorite." Glancing at her two best friends, Bess added, "I guess they're sort of like the three of us—a blond, a redhead, and a brunette. . . ."

She paused and listened as steel drums playing calypso music rang out into the tropical air, bringing the cove to life. Calypso was the resort's standard way of welcoming new guests. The girls watched as the visitors stepped from the seaplane onto the island and were greeted with flowers and tall, refreshing drinks. There were a young couple, a family of four, and two older ladies.

"No go." Bess sighed, collapsing back onto her lounge chair.

"Maybe they'll be on the next plane," Nancy said hopefully. She watched absently as Steven Gibbs, the tall, blond owner of Pineapple Grove, strode toward the landing to personally welcome his guests.

George had opened one eye to watch the welcoming ceremony. "I read in a magazine that everything Gibbs touches turns to gold. Apparently, this land was just isolated jungle until he bought it. But he's turned it into this fantastic resort."

Nancy nodded. "They're not kidding when they call Pineapple Grove a 'slice of paradise,'" she said, quoting the resort's slogan. "As far as I'm concerned, there's only one thing missing."

"I bet you wish Ned were here," Bess guessed correctly.

Ned Nickerson, Nancy's boyfriend, was busy with his studies at Emerson College, near the girls' hometown of River Heights. Just thinking about him, Nancy felt a familiar warm rush.

"I miss him," she admitted. "But there was no way he could get away in the middle of a term."

Her mind still on Ned, Nancy watched distractedly as the new arrivals gathered around Steven Gibbs and his staff. The music had stopped while Gibbs addressed the group. Nancy was too far away to hear what he said, but she did catch an occasional ripple of laughter from the small crowd.

"Gibbs really has a way with people," Nancy observed. "I was impressed with him when he came to greet our plane yesterday."

"He does make you feel welcome," George agreed.

The girls heard a round of applause, then saw the group begin to disperse. Bellhops gathered up the luggage and guided the new guests toward the flower-lined path that led to the lobby.

Pineapple Grove had been built in the shape of a starburst. At the center was the main lobby, a huge glass dome that covered the round reception area, providing guests with spectacular views of the grounds and sea. Fanning out from the lobby were pastel-colored stucco buildings, two stories high and with terra-cotta roofs. These were where the guests stayed. Between the guest buildings were mazes of gardens, hot tubs, dining terraces, and thatched-roof huts that housed everything from small shops to kitchens.

From the map of the resort which was in their room, Nancy knew that Pineapple Grove had been built on a hooked, isolated peninsula of St. John. The hook was surrounded on one side by high, rocky cliffs that formed natural protection for the sandy beach and calm bay waters where the girls now lay. A narrow, curving road was the only link to the rest of St. John.

"It sure is a scorcher," George said, tugging a visor over her short, dark curls.

"Let's get something to drink before lunch," Bess suggested, looking for a waiter. The resort swarmed with helpful staff members, and their casual uniforms of turquoise print shirts and crisp white shorts made them easy to spot. Bess waved at one who was making his way down the beach. "I'm dying to try a coconut cooler!"

The waiter had just returned with their drinks when Nancy noticed Steven Gibbs strolling down the beach. He was escorting a petite woman who was wearing a red swimsuit and a matching wraparound skirt. Her features were nearly hidden by sunglasses and a straw hat that she had cocked over her face.

"Here comes our host." Nancy nodded toward the couple. "Maybe he can fill you in on the Hot Rods' arrival."

"Who's that woman with him?" Bess asked curiously. "She seems awfully familiar, doesn't she? Like maybe a movie star or famous model."

Sipping her cooler, Nancy idly watched as Gibbs found the woman an empty lounge chair not far from them. "You know, she does look familiar," Nancy said. "I just can't place her, though."

The resort owner brushed the sand from the chair and gestured for the young woman to sit. He was just about to leave when Bess called to him.

"Mr. Gibbs!"

He turned toward the girls. "Call me Steve, please," he insisted, flashing them a dazzling smile. "We're all very casual around here. And your name is . . ."

6

"Bess Marvin," she supplied. Then she introduced Nancy and George.

"Of course," Gibbs said. "I never forget a face—especially such lovely ones! You arrived on the launch from Saint Thomas yesterday, right?"

"Right." Bess was beaming. "We were wondering when Woody and the Hot Rods are going to arrive. The rumor that they're shooting a rock video here *is* true, isn't it?"

"Yes. The Hot Rods are coming." Gibbs pushed his hands into the pockets of his crisp linen suit. Despite the late-morning heat, he looked cool and energetic. "But don't tell me you came to Pineapple Grove just to see a rock band," he teased. "Don't we have anything else that might interest you? Snorkeling? Waterskiing? Maybe a shopping trip or two?"

"We're going out on the glass-bottom boat to check out the reef after lunch," Nancy told him. She didn't want the owner to think that they didn't appreciate all the great activities Pineapple Grove had to offer.

"And I'm sure I'll go waterskiing at least once a day," George added.

Gibbs smiled at them again. "Well, that's more like it. I'm sure you'll find that the more you explore Pineapple Grove, the more you'll find to keep you busy."

"Nancy's a pro when it comes to exploring," Bess explained. "She's a detective."

"Really? I didn't realize we had a detective in our midst," he said, glancing at Nancy. "I hate to disappoint you, but I'm afraid you won't find any mysteries here. Just—paradise."

Nancy was impressed with Gibbs's style. He made it look as if running a resort with hundreds of guests was the easiest thing in the world. And he certainly had the knack of making every guest feel special.

"I have to get back to my office," he went on, his blue eyes sparkling. He leaned over and winked at Bess. "I can see you won't be satisfied without a scoop. Between you and me, the guys are supposed to arrive some time today." Gibbs excused himself and headed for the main lobby of the hotel.

"Wow! I can't believe they're really coming," Bess exclaimed.

"I wonder if the rumor about the band is true," George said.

"You mean all the talk about them breaking up?" Bess toyed with the paper umbrella in her drink. "I can't imagine it."

"According to the newspapers, they have an iron-clad contract," Nancy said. "Even if they split up, they're locked into a recording deal with the same label. They could end up in a messy legal battle for years."

"Well, I'd never get over it if they broke up," Bess said dramatically. "They're the best rock group of all time."

"That's a bit of an exaggeration, isn't it?" someone said from outside their group.

The girls turned, and Nancy noticed that the woman in the red swimsuit had lifted the brim of her hat and was taking off her sunglasses to peer over at them. She seemed annoyed by Bess's comment.

"I'm sorry. I didn't mean to eavesdrop," the woman said, her expression softening.

"Oh, that's okay," Bess told her. "I suppose I *was* gushing—just a little."

As the woman took off the huge hat and fanned herself with it, Nancy recognized her delicate face and honey-blond hair. "You're Courtney Brooks," she said. "The singer."

"Courtney Brooks!" Bess echoed in a thrilled voice. "I *knew* you looked familiar. I must have seen your latest video a million times."

Courtney's brown eyes seemed to warm up at Bess's praise. "It's always nice to meet a fan," she said. "All I've heard about lately is how wonderful Woody and the Hot Rods are," she added, frowning again.

"Don't you like their music?" George asked.

Courtney's expression darkened. She leaned forward as if she were on trial and trying to convince a jury of her innocence. "It sounds like you know about the Hot Rods," she said. "So I guess you've heard the rumor that I'm the one responsible for the band's breakup."

9

Chapter

Two

BUT DOES THAT MEAN that the Hot Rods are really going their separate ways?" Nancy asked the blond singer.

Now that she thought about it, Nancy did recall reading an article that blamed Courtney for the band's problems. It said that the musicians had been at odds ever since the Hot Rods' lead guitarist, Woody Neal, began dating their former singer, Courtney. The other guys in the band claimed that she was interfering with business.

"I have no idea what's going on with the band," Courtney said, shaking her head. "See how ridiculous the press can be? I'm accused of tearing the guys apart, but the truth is, I haven't

10

seen or spoken to Woody for weeks." She bit her lip and stared out at the sea.

Courtney seemed a bit distant, but she had a candid quality that Nancy liked immediately. It was obvious that her situation with Woody was bothering her, and Nancy couldn't help feeling sorry for her.

"Did you come to Pineapple Grove to be in their video?" George asked after an uneasy silence.

Courtney shuddered. "I wouldn't be caught dead in a video with those guys. I met Steve Gibbs at a party a few months ago and he asked me to sing for the opening of the Coral Cove—a new nightclub here. I didn't find out until last week that the Hot Rods were going to be here at the same time. I nearly canceled, but I had a contract, and also I didn't want to leave Steve in the lurch."

Nancy nodded sympathetically. She could imagine how uncomfortable it would be for Courtney to be stuck in the same place as her ex-boyfriend—plus his entire band. Pineapple Grove may be a tropical paradise, Nancy thought, but it was obviously the last place on earth Courtney Brooks wanted to be just then.

"That was delicious," George said, munching a piece of coconut from the lunch buffet. "I've never seen so many tropical fruits in one place."

The girls were just finishing up a lunch of chilled lobster salad and juicy pineapple, melon, banana, oranges, and mangos.

"I could sit here and eat forever!" Bess raved, popping another piece of coconut in her mouth.

"Too bad we don't have that long," Nancy reminded her, checking her watch. "The glass-bottomed boat leaves in five minutes."

George slung her camera around her neck, and the girls headed down to the boathouse. One by one the passengers stepped from the dock into the wide, flat boat. Its sides were lined with benches, and an orange canvas awning shielded the passengers from the sun. The tall, wiry guide, who introduced himself as Vincent Lanchester, was the last one on.

"Everyone aboard?" he asked. After jotting down everyone's names, Vincent gestured to the north end of the bay. "We're going out over the reef," he explained. "Many fish feed and hide near the coral, so you'll have plenty to look at. They seem very fond of our glass boat. Maybe to them we're a floating people zoo."

Amid a chorus of laughter, Vincent revved the outboard motor, and they were on their way. As they cruised over a sandbar, the boat cut into a wave and saltwater whipped over the side, spraying Nancy and the dark-haired girl sitting beside her. Nancy laughed, enjoying the wet coolness of the water on her sun-soaked skin. The other girl let out a squeal of surprise.

Nancy introduced herself, and learned that the girl's name was Eva Rivera. Eva seemed to be shy, so Nancy tried to make her feel at ease. She learned that Eva was from Mexico, and that she had just arrived at the resort that morning.

"That's funny," Bess chimed in. "I didn't see you arrive—and I thought we had the only port of entry covered. We've been watching for Woody and the Hot Rods," she confided.

Nancy noticed that Eva seemed to be unsettled by Bess's remark. The girl quickly glanced away, then looked back at Bess and asked, "The Hot Rods? You mean the rock band?"

When George explained that the group would be filming a rock video at the resort, Eva's brown eyes sparked with interest. "They are *very* popular in Mexico."

"Why don't we make a deal," Bess suggested. "Whoever finds the Hot Rods first will get the others, so that no one misses out on anything. Sound okay to you? We can meet tonight for dinner."

Eva nodded eagerly, then exchanged her room number with the girls.

They all turned their attention back to the boat as it glided into the darker waters of the coral reef. Vincent cut the engine, and everyone focused on the world beneath the Plexiglas hull of the boat.

First Vincent pointed out different types of

coral, including a patch of fire coral. "It can hurt you if you touch it," he explained.

"What about sharks?" someone asked.

"We don't see them in the Caribbean," Vincent answered, smiling. "Our water is too warm for them—like a hot bath," he joked.

Nancy laughed along with the crowd as Vincent fielded their questions with a dry sense of humor.

"Look there—that's a poey." Vincent pointed to a brilliant yellow fish with blue streaks on its face. "We call it a golden hamlet."

Nancy leaned forward to get a look at the brightly colored fish that darted between clusters of coral. A moment later a fiery orange grouper with spiked fins lingered beneath the hull, and Nancy heard George snap a picture beside her. There was so much to look at that the time passed quickly, and when the boat turned back toward shore, Nancy was surprised to see that it was after four o'clock.

Looking back toward land, Nancy noticed a chain of tiny islands at the mouth of the bay. The mountainous clumps of rock and trees seemed deserted. "Does anyone live there?" she asked Vincent, pointing.

"The Devil's Chain?" Vincent said, turning his eyes toward the rocky islands. He shook his head. "Those islands are uninhabitable. The rocky coasts make it difficult to get there by boat. And they are surrounded by cliffs with mazes of underground caves. Very dangerous." A dark frown came over his face. "There are stories of people falling into hidden passages and never getting out. That's how the islands got their name. Some people say the caves lead to hell itself!"

"Gee. A real hot spot," George said, teasing.

Beside her, Bess was shivering. "Sounds pretty creepy to me," she put in.

When the boat reached the dock, George insisted on a group photo. "Let's get a picture with Eva."

"I'll take it," Nancy offered. Lifting the camera to her face, she stepped back and focused. "A little closer together—that's it. Now smile and say—"

Just as Nancy was about to snap the shutter, something obscured her view. The camera had been ripped from her hands and thrown to the ground!

Stunned, Nancy stared at the camera lying in the sand, then at the dark-haired man who'd knocked it out of her hands. He was in his forties or fifties and was panting as if he'd run across the beach just to knock the camera out of her hands.

"What did I tell you?" he growled at Eva, his face a bright red that almost matched his striped red and white swim trunks.

"But, Papa, they are my friends," Eva explained, tears glimmering in her dark eyes.

Nancy felt a rush of anger. Not only had Mr.

Rivera rudely knocked George's camera to the ground, now he was humiliating his daughter. She didn't see what the big deal was. It was only a picture. . . .

Mr. Rivera said something to Eva in rapid-fire Spanish. With downcast eyes, she turned and ran up the flower-lined path toward the hotel.

George picked up the camera and brushed a clump of sand from it, and Eva's father paused to ask in a harsh voice, "Is it broken?"

George peered through the lens, then snapped a random picture. "I don't think so."

With a brisk nod, he turned and marched back to the hotel.

"What a grouch," said Bess, her pale blue eyes following Mr. Rivera's retreating back.

"Looks like we got Eva in trouble," Nancy said thoughtfully, "though I can't imagine what we did to make her father so angry."

"That's the fifth outfit you've tried on, Bess," Nancy said, glancing down at the clothes strewn over her friend's bed.

The girls had all showered after returning to their room, and Nancy was now in a white linen sleeveless dress that showed off her new tan. George had on yellow shorts and a colorful Hawaiian shirt. Now the two girls were sitting on Nancy's bed, watching the pile of discarded clothes on Bess's bed grow.

"It's a good thing we're just going to dinner,"

George cracked to Bess. "If this were a special occasion, it would take you until the end of our vacation to find an outfit!"

"But it *is* a special occasion," Bess insisted, fussing with the belt of a green silk dress and looking at her reflection in the full-length mirror on the outside of the bathroom door. "I have to look my best. Word has it that the Hot Rods will be arriving any minute!"

Getting up from the bed, Nancy said, "Well, let me know when you're ready to make your debut. I'm going to wait out on the balcony."

Outside, the trade winds, gently rustling through the palm trees, lifted the ends of Nancy's reddish blond hair. She was glad to have a room on the second story because the balcony overlooked one of the rocky sea cliffs, and the view was breathtaking. Leaning on the balcony railing, she could see pretty, thatched-roof huts and gardens as well as the sea and the full moon that now hung low in the darkening evening sky. The scent of roses and hibiscus and jasmine filled the air, mixing with the salty freshness of the sea.

As Nancy stood there gazing out at the dark horizon, a sudden movement caught her eye. The shadowy figures of three men emerged from a thatched-roof hut near the edge of the cliff. Peering at the small stucco building, Nancy saw that it had no windows. There was one door that she could see, and the far side of the hut seemed to be wedged right against a cluster of rocks.

With the help of the moonlight, she could make out the three men fairly well. Nancy could tell, from his uniform, that one man had to be a resort employee. The other two were wearing suits and carrying luggage. They appeared to be young and good-looking, with dark hair.

Nancy followed their progress until they disappeared around a bend. What were they doing coming out of a hut without windows? she wondered. Hotel guests wouldn't be staying in a place like that. She turned as George stepped out onto the balcony behind her.

"I think Bess has narrowed it down to two dresses," George said, sitting down in a wicker chair, the hotel guidebook in her hand.

"Does that guide have a map of the resort in it?" Nancy asked.

"Sure." George handed the book to Nancy. "What are you looking for?"

"I'm just curious about that hut near the edge of the cliff." Nancy's finger traced the area of the map until she found the small building she was looking for. "This says that it's a maintenance shed, but I just saw some guys coming out of it with their arms full of luggage."

"That's strange," agreed George. "Are you sure you've got the right spot on the map?"

Nancy was about to check the map again when Bess appeared on the balcony. "Tah-dah!" she announced, making a pirouette to show off her black linen miniskirt and sleeveless red top. "Ready!"

"Great!" George jumped out of her chair. "Quick, Nancy. Let's go before she changes her mind again."

As they left their room, Nancy asked, "Do you mind if we drop by Eva's room first? I'd like to smooth things over with her father if we can."

"That's a good idea," George said. "She's staying in this wing of the hotel. Room 108."

The girls went down the stairs and found the Riveras' room on the first floor. As Nancy knocked on the door, it swung open.

Surprised, she called out, "Hello? Eva?" and peered inside.

"Can I help you?" A smiling maid appeared in the doorway of the bathroom. She was holding a stack of fresh towels.

"We were looking for our friend, Eva Rivera," Nancy said, stepping into the room, Bess and George right behind her.

"Rivera," the woman said, shaking her head. "No, she's checked out."

"Checked out?" Bess asked, looking confused.

"But she and her father just arrived this morning," George added.

Nancy shared her friends' surprise. Why would Eva and her father leave the resort after just one day?

Chapter

Three

Nancy TRIED to ask the maid some more questions, but it was obvious the woman didn't know any of the details. Feeling disappointed, the girls left.

"It's a shame about Eva," George said as they walked past a fountain in the main lobby. "Maybe there was a family emergency."

"Maybe," Nancy said. Still, something about the girl's sudden departure—and Mr. Rivera's outburst on the beach—bothered her. Nancy paused and glanced at the reception desk.

"Why don't you two go ahead and save me a place," she suggested. "I just want to check here to see if the hotel has some information about why the Riveras left."

The woman at the front desk was polite and

efficient. After Nancy explained the situation, the receptionist turned to the keyboard of the hotel's computer and entered Eva's name. "There was a Rivera registered here," she told Nancy after a moment. "They checked out late this afternoon."

"But they just arrived this morning," Nancy explained. "Do you know why they left so soon?"

The woman shook her head. "I'm sorry, miss. My shift just started twenty minutes ago, so I wasn't here when they checked out. But short stays aren't really that unusual."

Nancy frowned. Why would someone take the trouble of flying to the Caribbean for a single day? It didn't make any sense. Looking at the woman behind the reception desk, Nancy asked one more question. "Can you please see if she left a message for me and my friends? She was supposed to meet us this evening."

The receptionist checked the computer again but found nothing. Frustrated, Nancy thanked the clerk and turned away. The lobby was lined with desks for representatives from airlines, travel agencies, and taxi services. When Nancy noticed a man in a khaki-colored uniform sitting behind a desk labeled Carib Air Taxi, she walked over to him and asked if he knew anything about the Riveras' sudden departure.

"I may have seen the girl you're looking for," the man told her. "I was on duty for our four o'clock flight. And I think I do remember your friend—Rivera, you said, right?"

Nancy nodded. "Did you happen to learn why they were leaving?"

The agent shrugged. "I'm afraid not, miss. There was no time to chat with your friend and her father. They booked late. Actually, they almost missed the flight. They rushed in and boarded the plane at the last minute."

Nancy couldn't be positive, but it seemed as if the Riveras had intended to stay longer but for some reason had changed their plans. Surely Eva wouldn't have agreed to meet them that night if she had known she was going to be leaving. Why, then, had they left?

Nancy shook her head. She was sorry that Eva was gone, but that didn't mean anything terrible had happened. Pineapple Grove was a busy resort, and people did come and go every day. She decided that her detective's imagination was running away with her.

Thanking the booking agent, she stepped away from his small desk. A crowd had collected in the lobby, and Nancy noticed a flurry of excitement around the reception desk. Huge black amplifiers and cases of sound equipment were stacked against one wall of the lobby.

Nancy grinned. It looked as if the Hot Rods had finally arrived. The blond guy leaning over the check-in desk certainly looked like Tucker Dawson, the band's drummer. The squeals and shrieks of some teenage girls who'd collected in the lobby confirmed it.

"Look! It's Tucker Dawson," shouted one girl.

"Can I have your autograph?" a freckle-faced girl asked, rushing up beside the drummer. "I'm your biggest fan. Really and truly!"

Suddenly everyone in the lobby was rushing over to the reception desk to catch a glimpse of Tucker. Nancy thought of running to get Bess and George, but she realized that the guys would probably be gone by the time her friends made it back.

"Oh!" Something poked Nancy in the back, causing her to spin around. She found herself face-to-face with a cute red-haired guy dressed in a red cotton rugby shirt, plaid shorts, and worn leather Docksiders.

"Sorry," he said. "Didn't mean to run into you with my violin case." He gestured at the black case that obviously held a guitar.

Nancy guessed right away that he was the band's leader, Woody Neal. "That's an awfully big violin," Nancy teased.

"Yes, well, classical music just isn't what it used to be." His smile was wholesome and carefree. "I'm Woody Neal, and this is my friend, Ricky Angeles." He pointed to a dark-haired guy who was propping his guitar case against a nearby rubber plant. Some fans had just come up and were hovering excitedly behind him. "He plays the oboe. And you are?"

"Nancy Drew." She smiled at the guys, enjoying the joke. "And I play the kazoo."

"Perfect!" Woody exclaimed. "We've been looking for a redheaded kazoo player. So tell us, Nancy, is Pineapple Grove really a slice of paradise, like it says in the pamphlets?"

"It's pretty close," Nancy admitted. Staring into Woody's sparkling green eyes, she could understand what Courtney saw in him. "There's swimming and snorkeling on the beach. And—"

She was interrupted when Tucker Dawson and the hotel clerk joined them. A handful of staff members were helping to keep curious fans from getting too close. Clearing her throat, the hotel clerk said politely, "Steven Gibbs asked me to extend his personal invitation to a party being held in your honor. It's at nine on the Palm Terrace. Can we count on you to attend?"

"Sure," Woody replied. Turning to Nancy, he said, "I hope you're planning on going, too."

Nancy hesitated for a moment. "I don't want to intrude. Besides, I'm here with two friends."

"Bring them along," Woody insisted.

"Don't think he's kidding," Ricky added. "He'll be devastated if you don't show up."

"And don't forget your kazoo," Woody called back over his shoulder as he turned to follow the bellhop across the lobby. "See you at the party!" He ducked through a doorway just as a new pack of girls entered the lobby.

"There they are!" cried a petite blond girl. "Don't lose them!"

Shaking her head, Nancy darted off to the

dining room to join her friends. When Bess heard about the party, she was going to be in seventh heaven!

"Everything looks so romantic," Bess said, seated at a table on the terrace a couple of hours later.

Nancy had to agree. The rooftop terrace was softly lit with tiny white lights strewn through the palm trees and ~~table~~top candles in hurricane globes. Taking a sip of her fruit punch, Nancy watched other guests wait their turn to speak to the band members.

"That's Enrique Angeles. Everyone calls him Ricky. He plays the bass," Bess explained to no one in particular. "People say he's the soul of the band. And that ~~tall~~, gorgeous blond is the drummer, Tucker Dawson. He's the one I'm dying to meet." Bess's blue eyes became glazed and dreamy-looking as she stared at the drummer. "I can't wait to go over and meet them, but there are still too many people."

After a while the crowd around the band began to thin out, and Nancy saw the Hot Rods begin to wander through the terrace, stopping now and then to talk to fans and sign autographs.

"Now's my chance," Bess said excitedly. But before she could even stand up, she added in a shrill whisper, "I don't believe it—they're coming over here!"

Turning in her rattan chair, Nancy saw that

Woody had spotted her and was waving. She waved back, and he jogged over to the girls' table and squeezed a chair in between Nancy and George.

"It's Nancy Drew and her kazoo-playing friends," Woody teased. "Listen, you guys have got to bail me out. I'm being attacked by a pack of mad fans who want autographs for all their distant relatives. Mmm, those look great." He grabbed a couple of appetizers from the center of the table and popped them in his mouth.

"Woody Neal, meet my friends Bess Marvin and George Fayne," Nancy said with a smile.

"Hey, man," came a husky voice behind them. "Trying to keep all the beautiful girls to yourself?"

From the look of total amazement on Bess's face, Nancy knew the voice belonged to Tucker Dawson. Sure enough, when she turned, she saw the tall, solidly built drummer smiling down at them. After Woody introduced him, Tucker pulled up a chair next to Bess's. Nancy thought Bess would probably faint when he started talking to her about their new video.

Smiling, Nancy turned back to the others. Woody was talking to George. He stopped suddenly in midsentence to stare at something over Nancy's shoulder. He became distracted, and his joking mood vanished.

Nancy stole a glance behind her and saw Courtney Brooks, who was talking to Steve

Gibbs. He was whispering in her ear just then, and she was laughing. They seemed so close and cozy that Nancy wondered if there was something between them. From the brooding expression on Woody's face, Nancy knew that he wasn't exactly thrilled by the scene.

"Excuse me," Woody said suddenly. After pushing back from the table, he stormed toward the closest exit.

Tucker stopped talking when he saw Woody leave. Then he spotted Courtney. "Oh, no—not again," he grumbled. "That girl has plagued us ever since she started dating Woody."

"You mean Courtney?" George asked, following his gaze. "But I thought they broke up."

Tucker frowned. "Doesn't matter. Some old flames never die. What's she doing here, anyway?"

"She's the featured singer for the opening of the new nightclub here," Bess explained.

While Bess and George talked with Tucker, Nancy excused herself and went to get a glass of punch. On her way back to the table, she saw Courtney standing alone next to a thick oleander bush at the edge of the terrace. She was staring at the round orange moon.

The singer frowned when she saw Nancy. "Guess you think I'm a party crasher." Before Nancy could respond, she explained, "I saw Woody storm out." Courtney's hands were shaking, and Nancy could tell she was genuinely

THE NANCY DREW FILES

upset. "Maybe I shouldn't have come tonight. But I thought Woody and I could start fresh—at least be friends. Instead, the other guys will say it's my fault that Woody ran out of here."

"He didn't seem too happy about seeing you with Steven Gibbs," Nancy said.

"Steve?" Courtney seemed surprised. "Oh, we're just friends. I'd feel awful if Woody got the wrong impression about Steve and me. I wish I could make him understand how I feel."

Nancy looked at her curiously. "What do you mean?"

"I . . ." Courtney paused and took a deep breath. "I guess you could say that I'm still in love with Woody. He's a great guy, Nancy." Tears sparkled in her eyes. "But I'm *not* in love with his band, and while Woody and I were together, he would always take the guys' side instead of mine. He didn't trust me."

Nancy couldn't imagine what she would do if Ned didn't take her side and trust her. "I can see how that would hurt," she said sincerely.

"The other guys in the band never even liked having me around. They thought I was trying to butt in on their business decisions. In the end, Woody had to decide between them and me."

"It must have been a tough choice."

Courtney nodded, then sighed. "I suppose I'd better call it a night—before I cause any *more* trouble," she said with a bitter laugh.

Nancy watched as the blond singer made her

way through the crowd to the exit. It was a shame that Courtney and Woody couldn't resolve their differences, she thought, taking a sip of her punch. She leaned against the terrace railing to enjoy the view for a moment. This side of the Palm Terrace offered the same view of the cliffs and bay that the girls had from the balcony of their room, only the angle was slightly different.

A sudden movement below caught Nancy's eye. She focused on the spot and made out three figures, all coming out of the same windowless hut she'd noticed earlier. The figures were loaded down with baggage, just as the people she'd seen earlier had been. From that distance Nancy couldn't tell if they were hotel staff or guests, or even if they were the same people. She did notice something else just then—bright flashes of light were coming from under the door of the hut.

Nancy squinted, trying to get a better look, but it was too dark. What could be going on down there at that hour? It was after eleven.

She was about to return to her table when she heard a shuffle of feet just on the other side of the oleander bush she was standing next to.

"There you are," a voice growled.

"Good evening, Ricky." Nancy recognized the smooth voice of Steven Gibbs, but she couldn't see him or his friend. "You and the other guys in the band are enjoying yourself, I trust?" Gibbs asked.

"Don't humor me," the other one snapped,

and Nancy knew then it had to be Ricky Angeles, the Hot Rods' bass player. "You've been avoiding me all night," Ricky went on. "Stop trying to give me the runaround. I want to know what's going on—now!"

Nancy felt uneasy about listening to their argument. She had just decided to walk away when she heard Gibbs say, "Ricky, please, be patient. These things take time. She'll get here soon."

She? Gibbs's words rang in Nancy's head. Who were they talking about?

"I've waited long enough," Ricky snapped angrily. "Where is she?"

After a pause Nancy heard Gibbs say, "I told you, she'll be here soon."

Nancy shook herself, embarrassed that she had allowed herself to eavesdrop on so much of their argument. She was about to make a noise to let them know she was there, when Ricky's voice rose.

"Listen, Gibbs. You'd better make good on your promise, or I'll tell people what really goes on here at Pineapple Grove!"

Chapter

Four

"THAT WAS SOME PARTY," George said as she buttered a raspberry muffin the next morning. "I've heard of making a dramatic entrance. But last night everyone seemed to be competing for the most dramatic *exit.*"

The girls were eating breakfast on the main dining terrace next to the beach. A huge blue-and-white-striped canopy covered the entire area, offering guests protection from the sun as they ate from white wrought-iron tables.

"It was a bit like the plot of a soap opera," Nancy agreed. "I wasn't surprised when Woody and Courtney stormed out. But I didn't think Ricky Angeles was that high-strung."

"He's not, according to the press," Bess said,

spreading orange marmalade on a roll. "He has a reputation for being cool and easygoing."

Nancy took a sip of grapefruit juice. "He sounded pretty upset when he was talking with Gibbs. I wish I knew who the woman was they were talking about."

"Maybe she's a musician who's flying in to join the band," George suggested.

"That might explain some of the rumors about tension among the band members," Nancy said thoughtfully. "But why would Ricky get mad at Steve Gibbs about something like that? Gibbs doesn't have anything to do with the band."

"What if it's something romantic?" Bess said. "Maybe Ricky is planning a secret rendezvous with a beautiful celebrity, right here at Pineapple Grove."

Nancy nodded. "That's a possibility, too." She thought for a moment, staring out at the sparkling Caribbean. "I wonder how Gibbs met the Hot Rods in the first place?"

"Last night at the party Tucker told us that they'd never met Gibbs before yesterday," George said. "He said that Gibbs approached their agent and offered them the use of the resort for their video, probably just for the publicity."

Nancy buttered a slice of toast and took a bite. "That makes sense," she speculated out loud. "But the Hot Rods do seem to have some secrets. Ricky was really fired up about something last night. I wonder what he meant when he threatened to reveal what's going on at Pineapple Grove."

At that moment Nancy noticed Courtney Brooks standing at the head of the buffet line with a plate of fruit in one hand and a cup of coffee in the other. Nancy waved, and the singer walked over to join the girls.

"I have to eat and run," Courtney said apologetically. "I have a rehearsal this morning."

"I'm going to a rehearsal, too," Bess said, blushing. "I ran into Tucker in the lobby, and he invited me to watch the Hot Rods rehearse in the gazebo. He's so adorable. Now that I've met him, I'm crazier about him than ever."

"I'm glad you got to meet the guys in your favorite band," Courtney said. Nancy was relieved that Bess's mentioning the Hot Rods didn't seem to bother Courtney.

"Actually, we were just discussing them," Nancy told Courtney. "We were wondering about Ricky Angeles. He mentioned that he was meeting someone here—a girl—and we were wondering—"

"If he's dating anyone?" Courtney finished Nancy's question with an amused smile on her lips. "Not that I know of. But I'd be the last person Ricky would confide in. We never saw eye to eye. He always thought I was trying to steal Woody away from his precious band."

"Did you and Ricky argue about that?" Nancy asked.

Courtney shrugged and spiked a piece of pineapple with her fork. "Not really. *Tucker* and I went a few rounds. We used to fight like cats and dogs, but Ricky just went off and sulked when he was mad. He's quiet, keeps pretty much to himself."

Nancy frowned. That hardly sounded like the guy who was threatening Gibbs the night before.

"Unlike Woody," Courtney continued, "Ricky's definitely low-key. Don't you love his dark, exotic eyes? He was born in the Philippines, you know. Woody told me that Ricky's grandfather brought him to America when he was eight years old. His grandfather died last year, and I don't think he has any other family left. The guy lives just for his music."

Courtney finished off her coffee and ate the last forkful of fruit. "Sorry," she told the girls, getting up, "but I've got to run."

Nancy nodded as the blond singer dashed from the table. She was still wondering about Ricky's threat. "There is something strange going on here," she said, thinking out loud. "Last night at the party Ricky made an outright threat. If he's usually a quiet, easygoing guy, then something is really bothering him."

Bess shook her head. "I think he's just so much in love, he can't control his temper. I wonder who the mysterious *she* is?"

"Bess could be right on this one, Nan," George

added. "The guy is probably just crazy about some girl."

Nancy shook her head slowly. "I don't know . . . I just have this feeling there's a mystery here. A guy like Ricky doesn't toss off threats without good reason. Something's going on," she added decisively. "I just have to find out what it is."

"Uh-oh, I sense a new case," Bess said, wiping her mouth with a napkin. "Well, I don't know about you guys, but I'm not letting a case or anything else get in the way of going to the Hot Rods' rehearsal." She got up from the table. "Do you have plans?"

"Snorkeling this morning," George told her cousin, "and waterskiing this afternoon. It's about time we got some exercise."

"I could have guessed," Bess teased. "Well, I guess I'll see you before dinner." With a quick wave goodbye, she took off for the gazebo. "Catch you later."

Nancy and George went back to their room to change into swimsuits before heading down to the boat landing. They boarded the small motorboat that was used to taxi swimmers to various parts of the island's coral reef.

"You'll have to dive in teams," instructed the boat driver. "That way you can keep track of one another underwater."

George and Nancy looked at each other and

then at the two guys in their early twenties who were sitting across from them in the boat. "Want to be on our team?" she asked.

"Sure," one of the dark-haired guys said with a nod. "My name is Juan Cordero, and this is my brother Eduardo."

"Call me Ed," the brother said. The skin beside his warm brown eyes crinkled as he smiled at the girls.

Nancy found herself staring at the dark-haired Corderos as they all assembled their masks and air tubes. Something about the two young men seemed awfully familiar, but she couldn't quite place them. She was trying to remember where she might have seen them, when the boat's driver cut the motor and turned to the swimmers.

"For your own safety, stay close to the other members of your team," the driver warned them. "Each team will have to choose a captain who's responsible for getting everyone back to the boat in thirty minutes."

George's strong, athletic build made her a natural choice for the captain of their team. Glancing down at her wrist, George frowned. "I left my watch back in the room."

"That's okay," Juan Cordero said. "You can borrow mine." He unstrapped a black water-proof sports watch from his wrist and handed it to her.

A moment later the swimmers plunged into the

water, checked their lightweight gear, then submerged their heads under the waterline so that just the ends of their snorkels stuck out.

Nancy was delighted by the aquamarine-colored world underwater. It was incredible to be swimming among the brilliantly colored tropical fish. She caught her breath as a glittering school of silvery fish darted around her legs. Beside her, George pointed out three bright orange fish that looked as if they were playing a game of tag. Ed found a clump of coral that was shaped like a huge tree, and Juan moved through the water so calmly that the schools of tropical fish actually followed him around instead of swimming away.

By the time George motioned that their time was up, Nancy felt as if she'd seen a billion rare, colorful kinds of sea life.

"That was great!" George exclaimed as soon as she took out her mouthpiece. Turning to the Cordero brothers, who were climbing back into the boat, she said, "I can tell that you guys have done this before."

"We did a lot of snorkeling at home," Juan explained. "The beach was only a stone's throw from our home in the Dominican Republic."

"The Dominican Republic?" Nancy tried to remember her geography. "That's not too far from here, is it?"

Ed nodded. "It's in the Caribbean."

"Why did you come here for a vacation?"

George asked, climbing into the boat behind the brothers. "I would think you'd want to try something different, like skiing in the mountains or ice-skating."

Nancy noticed that Ed and Juan became uncomfortable and acted awkward. Ed played with the strap of his mask as he mumbled, "Maybe we will, someday."

Nancy and George exchanged a confused look. The brothers were obviously taken off guard by George's question, but Nancy didn't understand why. She didn't want to seem nosy, though, so she let the subject drop and climbed up into the boat to join the others.

It didn't take long for the Corderos to regain their good humor. While the boat cruised back to shore, Juan leaned over and asked Nancy and George, "Are you girls up for a sports challenge tomorrow?"

Watching George's face light up, Nancy said with a laugh, "If it has anything to do with sports, George will go for it."

"Good," Ed said, smiling at them. "Then we will meet you at the tennis courts tomorrow morning at ten. And let me warn you, we are very competitive."

George returned his smile. "So am I."

"The Hot Rods are going to start filming their video tonight in the dance club!" Bess came bounding into the room from her spot on the balcony as soon as Nancy and George got back that afternoon.

"They want the excitement of a live audience," Bess went on breathlessly, "which means that we could end up in the video! Can you imagine the faces of the kids in River Heights when they see us in the Hot Rods' new video?"

George stepped calmly past her cousin and went to hang her wet towel on the balcony railing. *"If* we get on camera, and *if* the segment isn't cut," she pointed out matter-of-factly.

Bess placed her hands on her hips and said indignantly, "How can you be so calm about it? Anyway, I have an in with the band, so I'm sure we'll be on it."

"An in?" Nancy repeated, raising an eyebrow. "I don't suppose that 'in' would be the awesomely gorgeous Tucker?"

From the way Bess blushed, Nancy knew she had guessed correctly, but all Bess said was, "You'd better hurry up and change. We can go straight to the club after we eat."

"We have lots of time." George held up her wrist and noticed the sports watch still strapped on her wrist. "Oh, no! I forgot to give Juan his watch back."

"Juan?" Bess wriggled her eyebrows. "I can see that you didn't waste the day, either."

George told Bess about the Cordero brothers. "They're nice guys," she finished, shrugging, "but I don't feel like dropping anything to be

39

with them. I guess I'd rather concentrate on having a good time at the resort than on dating."

Nancy's skin tingled from being in the sun, and all the day's exercise had made her hungry. It felt good to take a cool shower and dig into the dinner of broiled tuna and fresh salad that was served in the terrace dining room.

George searched the terrace with her eyes as they ate. "I was hoping I'd see Juan so I could return his watch," she said. "I hate to keep something so valuable. Maybe I'll stop by his room right after dinner, and I can meet you guys at the club after that."

George took off to find Ed while Nancy and Bess climbed the carpeted stairs to Pineapple Grove's dance club. The club was located in a stucco building next to the dining terrace. Thousands of tiny lights were strung across the side of the building, giving it a festive look.

"Do you hear that?" Nancy asked as they approached the entrance.

"Yes!" Bess smiled and began to snap her fingers to the beat. "It's the Hot Rods—and the crowd adores them. Obviously, they began a little early."

Inside, the large room was pulsing with excitement. The crowd was swaying in time to the music, clapping their hands. A few girls shrieked as Woody jumped high into the air at center stage.

Ricky Angeles stood in a second spotlight at the side of the stage, his dark eyes wide as he sang the harmonies to a rock ballad: " 'Will you take the chance? Come on and dance!' " Behind him, Tucker threw his drumsticks into the air and caught them without missing a beat.

"Isn't he fantastic?" Bess shouted, waving at Tucker and jumping up and down.

"They're all great!" Nancy agreed, clapping along.

One camera was pointed at the band. A second camera panned the room, filming the faces of the exuberant crowd.

"Over here!" Bess cried, smiling and winking for the camera. She clapped and swayed when the eye of the camera swept over them.

Nancy turned as she felt a nudge from behind. The crowd was opening to allow someone to enter, and Nancy saw that the late arrivals were Steve Gibbs and Courtney Brooks. Their arms were linked as they walked toward the stage. Gibbs was beaming, obviously delighted to have the Hot Rods performing in his club. With a grin, he watched the camera that was focused on the band.

Gibbs looked down at Courtney, then flinched when he lifted his eyes and noticed the second camera filming the audience. The expression on his face darkened instantly, and he elbowed his way through the crowd to lunge at the cameraman.

"What do you think you're doing?" Gibbs demanded, grabbing the cameraman by the arm and shaking him.

Nancy watched in surprise as the cameraman sputtered, "I'm just doing my job, man—"

The band stopped playing and the crowd fell silent as Gibbs tore the camera from the man's arms, knocking him to the ground. "That's enough!"

Chapter

Five

NANCY STARED at Gibbs, amazed. It looked as if he might hit the cameraman, but Woody jumped down from the stage and stepped between them, helping the man to his feet.

"Hey, what's your problem?" Woody asked, staring at Gibbs. Tucker and Ricky were right behind him.

Gibbs's blue eyes glittered furiously. He opened his mouth to shout again, then seemed to reconsider as he glanced around at the crowd, now ominously silent. Almost everyone was staring at him, and Nancy could tell that they were shocked by his outburst.

When Gibbs finally answered, his voice was clipped. "I can't allow you to film my guests."

With a snap of his fingers, he summoned a waiter and gave him quick instructions. A moment later taped music was switched on, and the camera operator was escorted outside. The mood of the crowd eased as people began to talk and dance.

Nancy and Bess pressed forward toward the stage, and heard Woody ask angrily, "So what's the deal, Gibbs? You invite us here to film a video, and then you assault our cameraman."

Nancy had been wondering the same thing, but Gibbs shook his head and said firmly, "That's not the case at all, Woody. Your agent understood that there can be no filming of our guests. Didn't she warn you? You're welcome to film any of the facilities here, but I can't have any of my clients appearing on tape. Many of them come to Pineapple Grove to get away from cameras and nosy reporters. I have to respect their privacy."

As he spoke, Nancy saw that Gibbs had regained his composure and was acting with diplomatic skill once again. "I'm sorry if I frightened you and your crew," Gibbs continued, reaching out to touch Woody's shoulder. "If you'll excuse me, I'll go apologize to your cameraman right now." He left the room, with Courtney following uneasily behind.

Bess stepped forward and tapped Tucker on the arm. "We can't be in the video? It's not fair."

"I'm afraid he's right," Ricky said sheepishly. "Remember how we talked about getting photo releases? Rachel agreed that there'd be too much legal paperwork involved. We can't use the tape we took tonight without getting a signature from every single person here."

"The guy had a point," Tucker agreed, "but he didn't have to manhandle our cameraman to prove it." He shrugged, turning to Bess. "I guess we're taking a break. Do you want to dance?"

As the couple went out on the dance floor, Woody turned to Ricky and said, "Gibbs may be right, but I still don't like the way he operates. Did you see the way Courtney followed him around? I can't believe she'd fall for a guy like that!"

"Take it easy, Wood," Ricky said in a low voice. "Don't let her get under your skin again."

"Look who's talking," Woody snapped. "You've been moody and unbearable since we got here!"

Ricky's dark eyes flashed with fury. Instead of answering, he unplugged his amplifier, grabbed his bass, and stomped out of the room. Still frowning, Woody started to pack up his guitar and amplifier.

Wow, tension in the band was high, Nancy thought to herself. But she didn't know how much of it was because of Gibbs and how much of it was infighting among the guys. Woody was definitely jealous of Courtney and Steve. Even though Courtney had told Nancy that she and Steve Gibbs were just friends, Woody obviously didn't believe it. And what was that blowup between Ricky and Woody all about? Nancy shook her head, overwhelmed by it all. Rock 'n' rollers sure did lead dramatic lives.

"Nancy!"

Nancy turned to watch George weave her way through the crowded dance floor. "The Cordero brothers are gone!" George exclaimed. "The woman at the desk said that they just checked out."

"But we're supposed to meet them tomorrow morning at ten," Nancy pointed out.

"And I still have Juan's watch." George waved the black wristwatch in the air. "This is getting a little creepy. It seems as if everyone we get friendly with around here suddenly checks out."

A frown creased Nancy's forehead. "People do cut their vacations short. But two times with two different sets of guests? I wonder what's going on?"

"I feel awful about Juan's watch," George said. "Why didn't he call our room to try to get it back before he left?"

"They may have been in a rush. . . ." Nancy's voice trailed off as she pictured the Corderos taking off with armfuls of luggage. Then the image clicked and she knew why they had looked so familiar when she met them on the boat. "That's where I saw them!"

George stared wide-eyed at her. "Saw who?" she asked.

"The Cordero brothers," Nancy answered.

"Remember how I thought they looked familiar?" When George nodded, she explained, "They resembled the guys I saw coming out of that hut the other night, the one with no windows. I wasn't very close, but I did get a glimpse of their faces."

George still looked skeptical. "Even if it *was* them, what does that explain?"

"I'm not sure," Nancy said with a sigh. "Anyway, they're gone now. It looks as though my mystery's over before it began." She turned to head for an exit. "It doesn't look as if the Hot Rods will play again tonight. I'm going back to the room to read for a while."

George started tapping her foot to the recorded music. "Okay. Why don't we go to the Jacuzzi later, say around ten?"

"Great idea."

Nancy returned to her room and opened her book but couldn't get past page five. Somehow, she kept on thinking about the Corderos. Had she just *imagined* that it was them coming out of that little hut? Maybe . . . No, her instincts told her it had been the Corderos.

By nine-thirty she still was on page five. After changing into her suit and grabbing her tote bag, she left a note telling George to meet her. Then Nancy left the room and started down the path to the Jacuzzi. It was just a five-minute walk, but there was a stop she wanted to make on the way.

It was time to check out the windowless hut that she'd seen from her balcony and the terrace.

When she got to the hut, she saw that it had been built right against the mound of rock at the edge of the cliff. The sign on the door read, Maintenance—Employees Only.

Nancy scanned the area to make sure no one was coming before she knocked on the door. When there was no answer, she reached for the knob and the door swung open to her touch. It was pitch-black inside. Fumbling in the dark, she found a small lamp and switched it on before shutting the door behind her.

The room was eerie in the shadowed light. The lamp she'd found was on a desk. There was also another desk and lamp, half a dozen bulky, odd-shaped items covered with tarps, and a small collection of hand tools hung on one wall.

Nancy lifted the tarp in the center of the room. Under it she found a white screen that a photographer could use as a backdrop, and a Polaroid camera with a flash. She wondered what purpose this equipment served at a resort like Pineapple Grove. Maybe it was where employees were photographed for file records or ID cards?

Checking under another tarp, Nancy discovered two file cabinets. All six drawers were locked. She was lifting another cloth when she heard the metallic sound of a doorknob turning.

Nancy froze. She glanced furtively around the shadowed room, but knew there was no time to hide. She barely had time to flip the tarp back over the files before the door swung open. Nancy held her breath as a tall man filled the doorway. Nancy saw him straighten as he noticed her.

When he spoke, his voice was a menacing growl. "What do you think you're doing in here?"

Chapter

Six

THE MAN was blocking her only way out of the room. Nancy took in his dark features and realized with a start that it was Vincent, who had piloted the glass-bottomed boat the day before. He'd been so easygoing and helpful on the boat ride—nothing like the cold, threatening person glaring down at her now.

When Nancy didn't answer his question immediately, he asked, "How did you get in here?"

"The door wasn't locked," she said uneasily. His probing stare made her uncomfortable, and her gaze drifted down to his hands, which were balled into tight fists.

Vincent shoved a hand into the pocket of his shorts and pulled out a round key ring. Nancy wondered if he had forgotten to lock the door and had returned to take care of it. That would explain why the door had been unlocked.

But at the moment Nancy had more important things to figure out—such as how to get out of there! It was time to play the bumbling guest and hope that he fell for it.

"Is this your office?" she asked innocently, fumbling in her tote bag. "I must have taken a wrong turn somewhere on my way to the Jacuzzi. Where is that map? I always get lost without it. This place has such a maze of buildings—"

"And you thought you would find the Jacuzzi in here?" Vincent snapped.

"No, I was just looking for someone to steer me in the right direction," Nancy answered quickly. "I saw my friends here the other night— Juan and Ed Cordero. Do you know them?"

Vincent shook his head, still watching her, but she thought she noticed a flicker of surprise in his dark eyes.

"Well, anyway"—she started edging toward the door—"I thought I might find them here again."

"You must be mistaken," Vincent grumbled. "This hut is used to store lawn mowers and tools."

Nancy sensed that he was hiding something, but she wasn't about to confront him at night in an isolated place.

As if he had read her mind, Vincent folded his arms and said in a low voice, "A pretty girl could get hurt around heavy equipment like this. That's why the sign says employees only."

Was that meant to be a threat or merely a warning for her own good? "I'll be more careful in the future," she assured him. With a hurried apology, she slipped past him and rushed down the path to the Jacuzzi.

"So, you were trapped with Vincent?" George asked after she joined Nancy and Bess in the hot tub, and Nancy told them about her encounter.

"I thought that guy was creepy when he told us those stories about the islands," Bess said, shivering despite the warmth of the water in the Jacuzzi. "What were they called again?"

"The Devil's Chain." Nancy sank deeper into the hot tub so that the bubbling water covered her shoulders. "Anyway, I got the feeling he was trying to hide something. He definitely wasn't happy to see me there. I just wish I'd had a chance to see what was under all the other tarps."

"What were you expecting to find, Nan?" George asked, pushing her wet, short hair off her face.

"I don't know exactly, but I'd be willing to bet that that fancy camera equipment isn't used for maintenance. The camera must have been used last night, because I noticed quick flashes of light coming from under the door."

"Maybe Vincent is hiding his camera from the boss," Bess suggested, giggling. "Gibbs is so camera shy that he'd probably fire Vincent if he saw him holding a roll of film."

Nancy started to laugh at the joke, but then stopped and said, "That's it. Cameras. A lot of the weird events at Pineapple Grove seem to involve cameras."

"Snap out of it, Nan!" Bess said, giving her a light splash. "What are you talking about?"

Nancy studied her friends seriously. "I think something is going on. I don't know what it is, but cameras seem to be a part of the mystery. First Eva's father wouldn't let us take her picture. Then Gibbs wouldn't let his guests appear on film. Then I find a hidden camera in the maintenance shed."

"But how could all these things be connected?" George asked, shooting Nancy a quizzical look.

"I'm not sure," Nancy replied. "But I think it may be worth investigating."

George lifted her hand out of the water and studied it. "We'd better get out soon, before we turn into prunes," she suggested, reaching for a towel.

The girls were on their way back to their room when they heard loud voices in a garden the path passed through.

"We've been through this a million times before," they heard a female voice insisting.

"You shouldn't be here," a man snapped. "Aren't you satisfied with the damage you've already done?"

Nancy recognized Courtney's and Woody's voices. Peering over a leafy hedge, she saw the couple sitting on the edge of an illuminated fountain.

"What damage?" Courtney scoffed. "I never did anything to hurt you."

"Oh, come on, Court. How do you think I feel when I see you with that guy?"

Courtney sounded weary as she replied, "I told you, Steve and I are just friends. I'm here to do a job, Woody. Do you really think I'd come here just to make you jealous?"

He hesitated, then turned away and covered his face with his hands. "I don't know what to think anymore."

"That's always been your problem," said Courtney. "You listen to your friends, to your agent, to the guys in the band. You let them dictate everything to you. When we started dating, you even had me cleared with the band. You never trusted me, Woody," she said, her voice trembling. "You never even gave me a chance!"

"Wow," Bess whispered. "She's really upset."

"Maybe we should just disappear," George mouthed.

Nancy nodded. The girls started down a path, but a moment later they realized it just doubled back to the fountain. This time they had a close-up view of the unhappy couple.

Woody raked his hands through his red hair. "Listen, Court," he was saying, "I'm not here to rehash all our old arguments. I just want to give you a piece of friendly advice. Steer clear of Steven Gibbs."

His voice rose on a new wave of anger. "If you get involved with that guy, I guarantee he'll cause you nothing but trouble."

Chapter

Seven

NANCY, BESS, AND GEORGE exchanged a look of surprise. Holding a finger to her lips, Nancy went back down the path, away from the couple, and managed to cut through to another path that led to the main lobby.

"Wow," said Bess as they made their way back to the room. "What do you think Woody meant?"

"About Gibbs?" Nancy asked, shaking her head. "I'm not sure, but I know one person who does. Steven Gibbs. Ricky was mad at Gibbs about something at the party for the Hot Rods. And now Woody's warning Courtney away from him, too. I'm beginning to wonder if his involvement with the band goes deeper than they're letting on."

Nancy snapped her fingers as she thought of something new. "Maybe Gibbs knows something about why Eva and the Corderos left suddenly, too. After all, he *is* the resort's owner, and he seems to keep track of everything that goes on."

Bess looked puzzled. "But he seems so charming and helpful. Just because he got mad about a camera doesn't make him a bad guy."

"That's true," Nancy agreed. "But I'm still going to talk to him."

The next morning, after a quick breakfast, Nancy went to Gibbs's office on the second floor of the dome-shaped central building. His secretary, an attractive black woman who looked as if she was in her forties, told Nancy that he was in a meeting but that she could wait if she wanted.

Nancy sank into a salmon-colored leather sofa across from the receptionist and began leafing through a magazine. She was just finishing an article when the door to Gibbs's office flew open and Ricky Angeles stormed across the reception area, his face flushed red. He passed only inches from Nancy, but he was so angry, he didn't even notice her sitting on the couch as he left.

Her brow furrowed, Nancy was wondering if his anger had anything to do with his fight with Gibbs at the party for the Hot Rods. But her thoughts were interrupted by the secretary's voice.

"Mr. Gibbs will see you now." Nancy looked

up to see the secretary gesturing for her to go into Gibbs's office. Two walls were glass and overlooked the gardens and beach of the resort. The floor was covered with thick, cream-colored carpeting.

"Good morning, Nancy." Gibbs greeted her with a warm grin from behind a large mahogany desk. "Are you and your friends enjoying yourselves here at Pineapple Grove?"

"Yes, everything's terrific, and we were really thrilled to meet the Hot Rods. In fact, they're the reason I'm here. I want to ask you a few questions about them."

"Questions?" Gibbs closed a folder that had been open on his desk and clasped his hands. "Don't tell me you've stumbled upon a case here at my resort."

Nancy wasn't sure what to answer. She was curious about the Corderos and Eva, and she did think something weird was going on at that maintenance hut, but she didn't exactly have enough evidence to call it an official case.

"Not exactly," she told him. "I was just amazed at our good luck to be here while the Hot Rods are filming their video. How did you happen to meet them?"

"Between you and me, I never met them until they arrived here, the day before yesterday," Gibbs admitted. "The entire deal was worked out with their agent, Rachel Meredith. I met her a few months ago in New York City. The band was scouting for a warm, picturesque place to shoot, and I was looking for advertising. When I realized that we'd have instant publicity if their rock video was filmed here, Rachel and I made the deal."

He seemed sincere, but Nancy couldn't help wondering if Gibbs was telling her the whole truth. If he had just met the Hot Rods, what caused the friction between him and Ricky Angeles?

Before she could ask him about it, Steve Gibbs continued in a wistful voice. "At the time it seemed like a match made in heaven."

Nancy noticed that his smile had faded, so she asked him, "Do you regret making the offer?"

"I wouldn't say that I regret it," he hedged. "The Hot Rods are welcome here, but my top priority is my guests. I can't let a bunch of rock musicians destroy their privacy."

"You mean the way their cameraman filmed the crowd last night?" Nancy asked. As far as she was concerned, Gibbs had definitely overreacted, but maybe he did have a point.

Gibbs's blue eyes were serious as he leaned across his desk. "I feel terrible about what happened last night because I hate playing the heavy. But there were people in that room who cannot appear on a nationally distributed tape. I have to protect the anonymity of our guests."

Nancy couldn't remember seeing any celebrities, and her curiosity made her ask, "Was there anyone in particular you were concerned about?"

Gibbs paused before responding to her question. "Let's just say that there are . . . well-known people vacationing here. Sons of movie stars, diplomats' daughters. I can't let anyone violate their right to privacy—not here at Pineapple Grove."

"I understand." Nancy nodded. "I guess success has its price. Your resort attracts the rich and famous, but they do need extra protection."

"Exactly." He flashed her a warm smile. "Any more questions, Madam Detective?"

"Just one. We met a teenage girl two days ago—a girl named Eva Rivera. She and her father left quite suddenly, and my friends and I were concerned. Do you know what happened to her?"

"Rivera . . ." He tapped his chin with his forefinger. "Oh, yes, I do remember now. I spoke with her father before they left. A family member had suddenly become ill. They had to cut their stay short to return home."

Nancy nodded. "That was too bad. What about Ed and Juan Cordero? They're brothers; they were from the Dominican Republic. They also disappeared abruptly."

"Disappeared?" Gibbs chuckled. "You make it sound so mysterious. The truth is, guests come and go every day. Still, I don't recall hearing anything about those particular guests."

After Nancy thanked him for answering her questions, she walked back to the room. She had to admit to herself that Gibbs's explanations made sense—but he hadn't explained everything, such as the argument he'd had with Ricky. Also, his style was so polished and professional, she guessed he could be putting on an act.

Letting out a sigh, Nancy realized that she hadn't really gotten anywhere. Her next step, she decided, would be to approach Ricky and Woody and talk to them about their suspicions of or involvement with the resort owner.

Back in the room, George was pulling a bright pink painter's cap over her dark curls. "There's a bike trip leaving in twenty minutes, and the Hot Rods are going along, so the cameras can get some footage of them in the countryside. Interested?"

"Sure!" Nancy said, reaching into a drawer for a pair of shorts. "I planned to go on one of those trips. The view from up in the hills is supposed to be amazing—and it'll give me a chance to spend some time with the guys in the band, too."

As Nancy pulled on her bicycle shorts, she told George about her conversation with Gibbs, and about the questions she still had about the Hot Rods' involvement with him. Pulling her hair high into a ponytail, she asked, "Where's Bess?"

"Off shopping with Courtney. Not even her love for the Hot Rods could get Bess on a bicycle," George said, grinning.

When Nancy was ready, the two girls went down through the lobby to join the other bikers, who were assembling on the circular drive outside. Two staff members were leading the trip—a jovial, burly man who introduced himself as Daniel and was handing out water bottles and helmets, and Vincent, who was in charge of assigning ten-speeds to the riders.

When Nancy got to the front of the bike line, she saw the spark of recognition in Vincent's eyes. He didn't say anything as he sized her up and handed her a bike.

Nancy gripped the handlebars and hopped onto the bike. She watched as Vincent chose bikes for George, Ricky, and Woody.

"Let's roll!" Woody said, pedaling backward on his bike.

Tucker pulled a helmet over his unruly blond hair, then flicked a thumb toward Woody, mumbling, "What a clown."

"I hope you guys are ready for a real workout," George said with a laugh. "I hear that the first half of the trip is uphill."

They all rolled their bikes into line as Daniel instructed the riders on the route. The first leg of the trip required steady exertion. Fortunately, the exercise would be offset by the gorgeous view. Tropical green forest rose steeply on one side, and the turquoise Caribbean sparkled below the rocky cliff on the other.

After winding steadily uphill for about half an hour, Nancy came around a curve to see Woody standing beside his bike at the edge of the road, looking out over a small cove that shimmered in the morning sun.

"It seems like there's a bay hidden around every bend in the road," she commented breathlessly, pulling up next to him.

"Yeah," Woody agreed. "Practically every inch of this place looks like it belongs on a postcard. It could be very romantic," he teased, wiggling his eyebrows up and down. "You know what I mean?"

Nancy laughed. She was flattered by Woody's attention, but she didn't want him to get the wrong idea. "It is romantic. I only wish my boyfriend were here to enjoy it."

"Uh-oh, I know that look. I can tell you're crazy about this guy. Why didn't he come along?"

"He's in school," she explained. "Ned's a student at Emerson College. It's in the Midwest, where we're from." Just talking about Ned made Nancy realize how much she missed him.

"A college guy, huh?" Woody glanced out over the water, suddenly thoughtful. "I guess you've heard about my romantic blues."

Glancing awkwardly at Woody, Nancy admitted, "I'm afraid it's worse than that. We happened to walk past you and Courtney last night on our way through the gardens."

"Oops." Woody grimaced. "I'm sure that wasn't a pretty sight."

Nancy shrugged. "Every relationship has its ups and downs." She didn't want to probe into anything that was none of her business.

"That's for sure." Woody frowned. "And I guess you could say that Courtney and I have hit the down part. It's bad enough that she's here on the same island, but when I see her with Gibbs . . ." He shook his head. "That guy is bad news."

Nancy studied Woody's serious expression and wondered again if his words were prompted only by jealousy, or by something more. "How long have you known Gibbs?" she asked.

"I just met him the other night at the party he threw for us."

"Then what makes you think he could cause trouble?" she persisted.

Woody raked a hand through his red hair. "I guess I don't think Gibbs is such a bad guy," he admitted, still gazing out at the water. "But he does have a reputation for living in the fast lane. He could break Courtney's heart without thinking twice." Woody became silent for a minute, and his forehead creased in a frown. "At the risk of sounding like the jealous boyfriend, I hate to think of her being hurt by that guy," he added quietly.

Nancy nodded sympathetically. Woody and Courtney seemed to care about each other, and it was sad that they couldn't work things out. At least Woody had answered one of her questions. It was jealousy—not some weird plot at the resort—that was at the root of his complaints against Gibbs. Maybe the friction between Ricky and the resort owner was being caused by something just as simple.

Then another thought occurred to Nancy. "Do you think that Gibbs could have anything to do with the negative publicity you guys have been getting lately?" she asked Woody.

"Oh, the rumors about the skeletons in our closets and all the squabbling between us?" Woody chuckled. "No, I'm afraid that we manage to generate those stories without any help from people like Gibbs."

Woody glanced down the road behind them to see if anyone was nearby. Realizing they were alone, he explained, "I'm afraid a lot of the problems between us are my fault. Tucker and Ricky got pretty upset when Courtney and I started seeing each other. She used to tour with us, and she and I ended up jamming together a lot. They were afraid I would split up the band to become a duo with Courtney."

"Was that your plan?"

His green eyes widened. "No! I was crazy about Courtney, but I'd never perform without the guys. We're a team. I was pretty ticked off that they couldn't accept her, but that's all behind us now. We're making this video, and we're supposed to go back into the studio to cut a new record in a few months. And speaking of videos," he added, turning his back toward the road, "we'd better get going. If we don't catch up to the camera crew, those two hotdogs will hog the video!"

Nancy and Woody pedaled to the summit of the hill, where they found the rest of the group resting and watching the video crew. Ricky and Tucker were trying to outdo each other with bicycle stunts in a grassy field. The ruins of an old stone mansion made a picturesque backdrop. The camera caught all the action, while the director shouted out instructions.

While Woody wheeled into the center of the group and started making faces for the camera, Nancy sat down in the grass beside George to watch. By the time the cameraman decided he'd shot enough, the sun was high in the sky.

"At least the trip back is mostly downhill," Nancy said as she swung onto her bike.

"But it's getting hot," George said, spritzing her face with a water bottle. "I can't wait to get back and go swimming."

"Great idea." Woody unstrapped the water bottle from his bike and squeezed, squirting Ricky in the face.

"Hey!" Ricky grabbed his bottle and aimed it at Woody. Others joined in as they began coasting down the road. Nancy and George were still laughing when they approached the first sharp curve in the road.

Daniel, who had handed out the water bottles at the start of the trip, shouted back to the group, "Careful on the curves. You'll pick up speed going downhill."

Nancy coasted ahead until she was beside Ricky. She wanted to talk to him about Gibbs, but hadn't had a minute alone with him so far during the trip. "Do you mind coasting so we can talk awhile?" she asked him.

"No problem. I'd rather go slow, anyway," he said, his eyes on the gravelly road. "These turns make me a little queasy."

They rounded the first curve, and Ricky's bike swept near the outer side of the road, sweeping pebbles aside. Nancy's stomach sank as she watched them bounce over the rocky cliffside.

"Take it easy," Nancy warned Ricky. For someone who was nervous on the turns, he was steering dangerously close to the cliff edge.

"I can't," he said, slipping ahead of her.

"What?" Nancy had to go faster to catch up with him. She shifted to a higher gear but still couldn't match his speed. "Ricky, slow down!"

"I can't!" he shouted, glancing back at her frantically. "I can't slow down. Something's wrong with my brakes!"

Ricky's bike shot down the road like a bullet. Nancy watched in horror as his front wheel hit a rock, sending the bike wobbling to the cliff side of the road again. Gravel and dust sprayed the air as Ricky skidded dangerously close to the steep precipice, then gained control only inches from the edge.

Nancy pedaled furiously to keep him in sight. Ahead, the road suddenly veered to the left. At the speed Ricky was going, he'd never be able to maneuver the turn. And the sheer drop over the edge led to a rocky cove hundreds of feet below!

"Nancy, help me!" Ricky screamed. "My bike is out of control!"

Chapter

Eight

THE WIND WHISTLED past Nancy's ears. She was going dangerously fast, but she didn't want to let Ricky get out of her sight. Nancy watched as he leaned forward, squeezing the brake grips even harder. It didn't help. He was still shooting toward the edge of the road—and the rocky cliff.

"Rub your foot against the tire!" Nancy shouted. She hoped he could hear, since the wind must have been roaring in his ears, too.

Nancy held her breath as Ricky moved his foot back and placed the sole of one sneaker against the tire. A screeching noise of rubber against rubber ripped into the air, but Nancy thought the bicycle slowed a bit. There was a thread of smoke, but Ricky kept his sneaker firmly against the whizzing tire.

Finally the bike slowed enough for Ricky to bring it under control. When he reached the bend in the road, he lowered one foot to the pavement and forced the bike to a spinning halt.

The brakes on Nancy's bike creaked when she pulled up beside him. Her heart was racing as she asked him, "Are you okay?"

"Yeah," he panted, getting off his bicycle, letting it clatter to the ground. Ricky's hands shook, and he doubled over, trying to catch his breath. He looked unharmed but was obviously badly shaken.

"I don't know what happened," he said to Nancy. "One minute I was riding along, talking to you—the next, I was ripping down the hill."

Nancy picked up Ricky's bike and examined the brake cable. It was severed. "You won't be using this bike again today." She showed him the ruined cable.

"How could that happen?" he asked, frowning. "Do brakes just wear down like that?"

Nancy shook her head. "Not usually. But there are signs of wear on the plastic casing around the wires."

Ricky's face had gone completely white, and he glanced nervously up the road behind them. "Do you think someone was trying to *kill* me?" he asked in a shaky voice.

Not wanting to alarm him needlessly, Nancy just said, "The cable was tattered, not cleanly

70

cut, so the brakes could have worn down naturally."

But she couldn't rule out the possibility that someone had tampered with the brake line. The wires could have been shaved down until the line was held together only by a thread. That way, the cable would snap under pressure, when Ricky was well on his way down the dangerous road. What she didn't understand was *why* anyone would do it.

While Nancy was checking Ricky's brakes, the other riders began to cluster around them. Daniel arranged for Ricky to ride on the back of one of the motor scooters. Nancy noticed that Ricky was still visibly shaken and kept shooting anxious looks over his shoulder, as if he were afraid something else might happen.

Vincent, who was bringing up the rear, arrived on the scene just after Ricky left on one of the motor scooters. Nancy quickly told him what had happened. When she showed him the tattered brake cable, Vincent seemed shocked. He immediately instructed all the other riders to stop and check their bikes before they could proceed. Then he led the remaining bikers down the hill.

"Whew," George whistled, eyeing the ruined cable. "No brakes on a twisting road like this? He could have been killed."

Nancy gave her friend a sidelong glance. "I

wonder if that was exactly what someone was trying to do."

"Poor Ricky!" Bess gasped. "Does he know someone is out to get him?"

"I think he's afraid of that," Nancy answered. She and George were filling Bess in on the details of the bike trip as the girls crowded in the bathroom to wash up for their late lunch. "But we can't be sure that someone cut the brake cables," Nancy reminded her. "It could have been an accident."

"Let's just say for a minute that someone *did* tamper with those brakes," George suggested. Wrapped in a fluffy towel after her shower, she was running a comb through her wet hair. "Who would want to hurt Ricky?"

Nancy's brow crinkled as she concentrated. "I don't know," she said. "The band seems to have its problems, but I don't think Tucker or Woody would do something that drastic just to get out of their contract. I talked to Woody just before, and he said he was committed to the band. But if he or Tucker *were* desperate enough, they would have had the opportunity."

"Not Tucker!" Bess insisted. She leaned forward to check her lipstick in the mirror above the sink. "He's the sweetest, cutest guy you'd ever want to meet. I mean, I know everyone's a suspect, but I sure hope it's not Tucker."

"Me, too," Nancy agreed. "I really like the guys in the band, but then we did see Woody argue with Ricky, too."

George headed into the bedroom to change. "And Ricky is definitely on edge about something," she called over her shoulder. "Even before the bike accident, he seemed nervous."

Nancy checked her pink T-shirt and white shorts in the mirror before following George back into the bedroom. "And then there's Courtney. She doesn't get along with Ricky or Tucker. In fact, Tucker didn't seem to like her at all at their party. He thinks she came to Pineapple Grove just to get in Woody's way."

"But Courtney couldn't have messed with Ricky's bike," Bess said from the bathroom door. "She was out shopping with me."

"True, but Courtney Brooks does seem to be at the center of many of the Hot Rods' problems." Nancy recounted what Woody had told her about the band's resentment of the singer.

"It wasn't her fault," Bess said emphatically. "She fell in love with Woody. The other guys should have understood that."

George smiled at her cousin. "Bess Marvin— sucker for romance."

"I keep thinking of Vincent, too," Nancy continued. "He was in charge of assigning the bicycles. He could have deliberately given Ricky a bike with worn brakes."

"But why would Vincent want to get rid of Ricky?" George asked. "They barely know each other."

Nancy shrugged. "It *is* kind of confusing," she said with a sigh. "And I'm too hungry to come up with any theories right now."

"Me, too," said George, tucking a short-sleeved knit shirt into her shorts. "Let's eat!"

When the girls reached the dining terrace, they went straight to the buffet table, which was still set up with fish and breads and tropical fruits.

Nancy scanned the outdoor terrace, then smiled and waved when she saw Woody. "Great, it looks like the band wants us to join them."

"We saved the seats of honor for our favorite female trio," Woody said as the girls arrived at their table.

"An adorable trio," Tucker said with a winning smile. He stood up and pulled out the chair beside him for Bess, who blushed as she sat down.

"He's right," Woody agreed. "Have you girls ever considered going into show business? Nancy and the Drewettes—has a nice ring to it. Can any of you carry a tune?"

"I love to sing," Bess volunteered. "And I'm a perfect soprano—in the shower."

Everyone laughed, then continued eating. Nancy was sitting next to Ricky, and she was relieved to see that he had recovered from his incident that morning. The color had returned to his face, but she did notice that the look in his brown eyes was strained and tired.

Leaning toward him, Nancy asked, "Are you feeling better?"

Ricky nodded. "But I'm still a little shaken up. Thanks for your help up on that hill today."

"That's for sure," Tucker agreed. "If it weren't for Nancy, our buddy could've been killed."

Woody nodded. "That was a close call. Thanks for keeping an eye on Ricky, Nancy."

"No problem," she said quickly, feeling embarrassed by the praise.

Nancy was polishing off a cookie later when she noticed that Woody's good humor had faded. His expression was hard as he stared at something behind her. Glancing over her shoulder, she immediately saw what had upset him. Steve Gibbs and Courtney Brooks had just sat down to lunch at the next table.

"Not again," Woody groaned, covering his face with his hands.

Tucker winced when he noticed Courtney and Steve. "Gee! I wish she'd get lost."

Beside Nancy, Ricky still seemed preoccupied. He looked distractedly at the couple for a moment, but didn't seem to see them. Then Nancy saw him fix on something with a sudden intensity.

"What?" Ricky's dark eyes narrowed as he stared. "I can't believe it," he said, jumping to his feet so abruptly that his chair fell back and clattered onto the flagstone floor.

"What's wrong, Ricky?" Tucker asked.

But Ricky didn't seem to hear the question. Red fury colored his face, and his fists were clenched as he pushed past the table and lunged at Courtney, reaching for her throat!

Chapter
Nine

As RICKY'S HANDS closed in on the singer, Courtney managed to push her chair to the side and jump up to avoid him. "What are you doing?" she screamed, her hand flying protectively to her throat.

Woody and Tucker jumped up and rushed over, grabbing Ricky and holding him back. "Take it easy!" Woody shouted. At the same time, Gibbs stood abruptly and tossed his napkin onto the table. "What's happening here?"

"He's crazy!" Courtney screamed. "Get him away from me."

"Let me go!" Ricky struggled in Woody's and Tucker's arms, but they managed to hold him back and away from Courtney.

"Where did you get those earrings?" Ricky hissed at her.

Her brown eyes were wide with confusion, and she touched the white stones in her earlobes. "They're new," she answered. "I just bought them at the hotel gift shop this morning."

Nancy had to admit she shared Courtney's confusion. Why was Ricky so uptight about a simple pair of earrings?

"I don't believe you!" Ricky snapped. He glanced back at his friends. "She's lying."

"She's telling the truth," Bess cut in. "I was with her when she bought them."

His eyes still glued to the earrings, Ricky refused to back down. Woody and Tucker did manage to calm him enough to lead him to an empty table on the other side of the terrace from Courtney and Gibbs. Nancy, Bess, and George followed.

Sinking down into a chair, Ricky hung his head in his hands. After a long moment he lifted his eyes, and the helpless look in them tugged at Nancy's heart. "I know you think I'm out of line," he said, "but I'd recognize those earrings anywhere. They were hand-carved in the Philippines, made of rare white jade. They've been in my family for years."

"How can you be sure?" Woody asked, touching Ricky's arm sympathetically. "There could be hundreds of pairs just like them."

"No," Ricky insisted, shaking his head somberly. "That design is very unusual. Courtney Brooks is wearing one of my family's heirlooms. They belong to my twin sister, Maria. Just before my mother died, she gave the earrings to Maria."

Nancy had gotten the impression from Courtney that Ricky didn't have any relatives, and she was surprised to hear about his sister. Turning to him, she asked, "Where's your sister now?"

"She still lives in the Philippines. When I saw Courtney wearing those earrings, I knew—" Letting out a deep sigh, he looked anxiously around at them. "I knew that Maria must be in trouble."

Nancy was more confused than ever. What was he talking about? And how could he possibly identify a pair of earrings when he probably hadn't seen them for years?

Apparently Tucker shared her doubts. "I don't know, man. You left the Philippines when you were, what—eight years old, right? That means you haven't seen those earrings for twelve years, and you think you'd still recognize them?"

"Yes," Ricky said firmly. "I emigrated with my grandfather when I was eight, but I went back to visit my sister last year. She was wearing the earrings when she saw me off at the airport. They're very distinctive. The design resembles a cluster of flowers—or a serpent, depending on how you look at it. You'll find my great-grandmother's initials engraved on the back of each post, J.A.—for Juanita Angeles."

79

Nancy rose from her chair. "Wait here a second," she said. "I'll go ask Courtney if she'll lend us the earrings so we can check."

She returned a few moments later with the earrings clutched in one hand.

"That's them," Ricky said without hesitation.

Up close the earrings were truly remarkable. Nancy was intrigued by the twofold design of flowers or a serpent, depending on the perspective of the viewer. Turning one delicate earring over, she examined the gold post. Sunlight twinkled on a rough spot, and when she looked more closely, Nancy saw the initials J.A. engraved in tiny letters.

"The initials are here, just as Ricky said!" she exclaimed. She checked the other earring and found the initials engraved there, too. Nancy's head was spinning. What were Ricky's sister's earrings doing at Pineapple Grove?

Turning to Ricky, Nancy asked, "Do you have any idea how Maria's earrings got here?"

For a second Nancy thought she saw a glimmer of fear in his eyes, but then he looked stonily down at the ground. "None. I just know that if she . . ." His voice trailed off.

"What?" Nancy prodded.

Ricky raised his eyes up at her, then shook his head and mumbled, "Nothing."

Why had he clammed up so suddenly? Nancy wondered. "Is there a way you can contact your sister?" she suggested. "Maybe call her on the phone and ask about the earrings?"

Again Ricky shook his head. "She lives in an isolated village—the nearest phone is miles away." He stood up to leave. "I'm beat. This whole thing has zapped my energy. I guess I'll head back to the room and crash for a while."

Woody watched sullenly as the bass player disappeared down the path. Turning to Nancy, he said, "Ricky's been like a zombie ever since we got here, but he won't talk about it, says he'll feel better once we finish the video. And now this happens. We're supposed to shoot part of the video in the gardens tomorrow, but if he's still like this, it'll be a total disaster."

"Do you think you can track the earrings down?" Tucker asked Nancy. "Find out how they got here? It might make Ricky feel better."

"I'll do my best," Nancy promised. Right then there were far more questions than answers in this case.

"What's the old saying about getting dragged into a situation?" Bess asked as she and Nancy walked through the main lobby. " 'In for a penny, in for a pound'? That's sort of what's happened to you on this case. First we were curious about the Hot Rods, then we thought something weird was going on here at the resort, then we got caught between the guys, Courtney, and Steven

Gibbs. And now we're trying to figure out how Ricky's sister's earrings got here."

The girls left the lobby and walked down a shaded path that led to an airy, stucco building where there were a number of boutiques. George had decided to join a snorkeling excursion for the afternoon instead of going with Nancy and Bess to the gift shop where Courtney had bought the earrings.

"I'm not sure if any of these things are related," Nancy admitted. "But those earrings are very important to Ricky, and he's definitely afraid that something terrible has happened to his sister."

"I'm glad you got Courtney to agree to give the earrings back to Ricky," Bess commented. Then she snapped her fingers. "Hey, I wonder if Maria is the mysterious woman Ricky was asking Steve Gibbs about the other night?"

"I was just thinking the same thing," Nancy said.

As the girls approached the gift shop, the glass door opened with a *whoosh,* and Nancy and Bess stepped inside.

"Can I help you?" asked a slender black woman behind the jewelry counter.

Nancy showed her the earrings, and the woman nodded in recognition. "Ah, the white jade posts," she acknowledged, glancing up at Bess. "And you were with the young lady who bought them this morning. Did the customer change her mind?"

Nancy explained that they were trying to track down the origin of the earrings. "Can you tell us when they were added to the shop's inventory?"

"We just acquired them last week," the woman answered. "I remember because Mr. Fitzroy—he owns the shop—boasted that they would sell quickly." She smiled. "He was right."

"Where did the earrings come from?" Nancy asked.

The woman tapped her nails on the counter as she thought. "I'm not sure. We get some of our jewelry from a U.S. distributor on the mainland, and some of the pieces are made by craftspeople on the island. But I'm only a salesclerk. Mr. Fitzroy buys our merchandise."

"Can we speak with him?" Nancy asked.

"Not today. He's taking care of some business in Saint Thomas. But he'll be here tomorrow."

Nancy thanked the woman and told her she'd be back the following day to speak with him.

As she and Bess stepped out into the sunny tropical day, Nancy paused to let the sun wash over her. "Mmm, this is perfect beach weather."

"Well, what are we waiting for?" Bess said, grabbing Nancy's arm and pulling her toward the building where their room was.

Twenty minutes later the girls were settled in lounge chairs on the beach at one end of the cove,

Bess in a yellow bikini she had bought the day before, Nancy in an aquamarine tank suit.

"Now, this is my idea of a vacation," Bess said, sipping a tall frosted glass of lemonade as she stared out over the blue-green water.

"It is great," Nancy agreed, "but I can't seem to really relax."

"Oh, Nan," Bess said with a yawn. She finished her lemonade and set the glass carefully down in the sand, then stretched out on the lounge chair and closed her eyes. "Once you start a case, you can never think of anything else!"

As Nancy watched a flock of herons circle the bay, she explained her plans to Bess. "I won't be able to go back to the gift shop until tomorrow."

"Thank goodness," Bess murmured.

"And then there's that maintenance hut, the one where the camera was," Nancy continued. "I want to go back and check that out again, but I have to wait until no one else will be there."

Glancing to her left, Nancy noticed that Bess had dozed off. Well, at least *one* of us is able to relax, she thought, laughing to herself. She swung her legs to the ground and stood up to take a walk on the beach. Strolling past the thatch-roofed refreshment stand, she climbed a small dune that had been created by the shifting tide, picking up shells as she went.

Nancy paused to look out at the water. It would be great if Ned were there to enjoy the resort with her, she thought. But Pineapple

Grove was still a pretty terrific place, she reminded herself, and she had plenty to keep her busy.

She was just reaching down to pick up an unusually thick purple and orange seashell when something just beyond the dune made her pause. It was a man, she realized, dressed in the turquoise and white uniform of the resort's employees. He was sprawled in the sand under a cluster of palm trees. At first Nancy thought he was catching a nap, but as she moved closer, she could see that his legs were twisted in an unnatural position.

Her pulse quickening, Nancy ran over to the man. A trickle of blood ran from a cut on his forehead down to the collar of his shirt. He was either unconscious or— She gasped when she saw his face.

It was Vincent!

Chapter

Ten

NANCY RUSHED up to the man and pressed her fingers against his throat. His pulse was weak, but he was still alive.

After jumping to her feet, Nancy ran down the beach to find a waiter. She quickly told the man what she'd found, and he rushed off to get help. Then Nancy raced for Bess, and together they hurried back over the dunes to where Vincent lay.

An ambulance was just arriving when they got there. As the girls watched, a nurse checked on Vincent and then spoke in low tones to Daniel, the burly staff member who had helped out on the bike trip.

"He's unconscious. Looks like a concussion or skull fracture. From a falling coconut, maybe, but we won't know for sure till a doc checks him out," the short, wiry nurse explained to Daniel as he and another medic lifted Vincent into the ambulance.

Daniel seemed to be nervous as he ordered, "Keep me posted." Then the nurse climbed in, slamming the rear door of the ambulance, and it drove off.

"Nailed by a coconut—imagine that," Bess said, whistling under her breath.

Nancy raised her index finger. "That's just one theory," she said meaningfully.

Daniel wandered up to them just then. His pudgy, usually jovial face was stony. "Vincent is lucky you found him, Nancy," he told her. "I am sorry your vacation was interrupted by such an unpleasant incident, but you may have saved our Vincent's life."

"Nancy's great in an emergency," Bess boasted. "That's one of the reasons she's such a successful detective."

"Detective? Well, thank you, Nancy. I don't want to keep you from your vacation any longer." Daniel took her and Bess each by an arm, taking several steps back toward the beach and their loungers. It seemed as if he wanted to get rid of them. But there was something Nancy had to find out first.

She disengaged her arm, turned to Daniel, and asked, "Do you really think a falling coconut could have hurt Vincent?"

"Without a doubt. It happens all the time." He pointed up at one of the coconut palms. "Those coconuts should have been harvested weeks ago. We usually pick them before they become over-ripe and fall. This tree must have been over-looked by our groundskeepers."

Nancy stared down at the dune. "But where *is* the coconut?" she wanted to know. All she could see was half of a hollow coconut shell and a dried palm frond.

"Maybe one of the guests picked it up," Daniel said irritably. He turned abruptly. "Now if you'll excuse me, I must make a report on Vincent."

"He didn't have to get so huffy," Bess said indignantly. "You were only trying to help."

Nancy frowned. "And I'm going to keep on helping, whether he wants me to or not. Come on. Let's talk to the other people on the beach. Maybe someone saw something."

They questioned everyone in the immediate area, but no one had seen a thing. For the rest of the afternoon, Nancy tried to relax on the beach, but she couldn't get the case, whatever it was, out of her mind. Now Daniel was acting as if he were hiding something, too. The Hot Rods, Vincent, Daniel, and maybe Steven Gibbs. They'd all been acting weird. Wasn't there anyone at Pineapple Grove who *didn't* have something to hide?

Nancy woke up early the next morning, eager to return to the gift shop. After a quick breakfast, she left George and Bess in the dining area and went to the stucco building that housed the boutiques. A pale, balding man was just unlocking the shop door when she got there.

"Mr. Fitzroy?" Nancy asked. When he nodded, she asked about the white jade earrings.

Fitzroy remembered them right away. "They were rather unusual, weren't they? I bought them from a resort employee. Normally I don't buy jewelry from people on staff, but the white jade was so special, I couldn't resist." With a quick flip of his wrist, Fitzroy turned to a page in the store's record book. "Here it is. I bought them from a man named Vincent Lanchester."

Nancy's blue eyes widened in surprise. Vincent! How did he get his hands on Maria's earrings? Nancy couldn't forget his connection with the maintenance hut, nor her feeling that he was involved with some kind of funny business being conducted there. The question was, how did Maria's jewelry fit in? Or did it?

Nancy thanked Fitzroy and left. Was it a coincidence that Vincent had gotten knocked out shortly after selling the earrings to the shop? Nancy supposed Vincent's injury could be unrelated to the earrings—or the weird activity in the dark hut—but her intuition told her that wasn't the case. The problem was, Vincent was the only person who could answer her questions about the earrings, and he was no longer around.

Nancy remembered promising to keep Ricky

informed about the earrings. The guys had mentioned that they'd be taping this morning, so Nancy headed there to give Ricky the latest news.

As soon as she got to the location, Nancy could tell something was wrong. Tucker and Woody were standing at the edge of a fountain, arguing with several members of the crew.

Spotting Bess and George, who were sitting on a nearby bench, Nancy went over to them. "What's wrong?" she asked. "Why aren't they taping?"

"World War Three just broke out!" Bess said, grabbing Nancy's arm. "One of the camera operators got spooked by Ricky's bike accident, and he says he'll quit unless they pack up and finish the video in L.A. The other cameraman wants to leave, too. After Gibbs almost punched him, I guess he'd be happier in L.A. than here in paradise."

"I can't say I blame them," Nancy said. "It hasn't exactly been smooth sailing for the video crew since they arrived."

"But Ricky flatly refuses to leave the island," George added, "and Tucker said that the whole film crew should be fired. The poor director's trying to smooth things over so they can keep shooting.

"Anyway," George continued, "the rumor is that one of the Hot Rods wants out of his contract so badly, he's sabotaging the video! But no one knows which band member it is."

Looking over, Nancy saw that although Woody and Tucker still looked harried, they were now talking calmly to the director and cameramen. Ricky was sitting a few yards away from them on a stone planter, tuning his electric bass. He wasn't looking at anyone, but the tension in him was obvious in the way he plucked at his guitar strings.

"What's up?" he asked as Nancy went over and sat down beside him.

"I found out who sold the earrings to the gift shop." When Nancy mentioned Vincent's name, she was met with a blank stare.

"Lanchester?" He shook his head. "I don't know who he is—do I?"

Nancy explained that Vincent had been one of the guides on the bike trip, and that she'd found him unconscious on the beach. Ricky's expression became grimmer, but he shook his head and said, "Still doesn't ring a bell."

He seemed to be telling the truth, but Nancy had the feeling that Ricky was holding back something important about his sister. She said, "Ricky, we have to try to figure out how he got hold of Maria's earrings. Has she ever visited Pineapple Grove?"

Ricky glanced away quickly. "I don't know how her earrings got in that guy's hands."

Again, Nancy had the feeling that he was hiding something. Before she could ask more, though, the director stood up, clapped his hands and shouted, "Okay, people, we're going to tape now. Take your places for the fountain scene."

"Got to run." Ricky looped his guitar strap over his shoulder and stood up. He seemed relieved to have an excuse to end their conversation. "Hey, Nancy," he added, "let me know when Vincent's available to talk. I'd like to speak to him."

Ricky pushed through the crowd to join the other two musicians on the edge of the fountain. Water spurted in arches behind them, making a glittering backdrop for them to be photographed against.

The guys plugged into their amplifiers, and the director began to shout instructions at the crew. The cameras began to roll.

"One, two—one, two, three, four!" Tucker shouted, and the Hot Rods burst into a song.

Immediately Bess started clapping along. "Doesn't that fountain look great behind them?" she shouted over the music. "You feel as if you could reach out and touch the water."

Nancy nodded, her eyes following the sparkling streams to the base of the fountain. Ricky had just started to sway in time to the music when she noticed something odd.

His amplifier was smoking! And the hot cord was swinging just inches above the water beside him.

With a gasp, she realized that Ricky was about to be electrocuted!

Chapter

Eleven

NANCY HAD TO break the flow of current before it killed him!

"Ricky!" she shouted. Maybe she could get him to drop the guitar before it was too late. Waving madly, she called his name again, but he obviously couldn't hear her over the music. When she finally did look her way, Ricky just nodded and smiled at her. He thought she was cheering him on!

Nancy looked frantically around for something to knock out the cord—something that wouldn't conduct electricity. Her gaze fell on a wooden croquet set, and she quickly grabbed a mallet and took off on a run to the fountain, pushing through the audience. Before she reached Ricky, however, he turned—the cord of his electric bass swung low and made contact with the puddle of water.

Sparks shot along the wire, and Ricky shrieked. There was a loud bang as his amplifier burst into flames. Lunging the last few feet, Nancy lifted the mallet and swung at the frayed cord. After two hits, the cord finally popped out of the amplifier.

Pale and listless, Ricky fell off the fountain and collapsed onto the ground. The other guys broke off playing and hopped down to check on him, shock and fear on their faces.

"Quick, call an ambulance!" Nancy yelled as she felt for his pulse. A medical team was on the scene minutes later. Everyone moved back as the attendants checked Ricky's vital signs and lifted him onto a stretcher.

As they carried Ricky out, Woody came over and slipped his arms around Nancy and George. "He's going to be okay," he said in a shaken voice.

Tucker joined them. "What would have happened if you hadn't been here?" he said to Nancy. "Ricky was almost killed!" He pulled a hand back through his thick blond hair. "I don't believe these incidents are accidents anymore. Someone is out to get us—or Ricky."

Nancy went over to the amplifier and picked up the disconnected cord. Its plastic coating was chafed away in a few places. "This doesn't look like normal wear and tear," she said, calling the others over. "There seem to be fresh cuts in the cord, probably made by a knife."

Woody shook his head as he examined the cord. "Ricky's equipment *is* new—he just replaced his amp system after our last tour. It was fine when we rehearsed yesterday afternoon."

"Who takes care of the band's equipment?" Nancy asked.

"Roadies handle the big stuff," Tucker explained. "But we take care of our own instruments and feedback amps."

Nancy reflected for a moment. "Is the equipment stored in a common place? A room that lots of people have access to?"

Tucker shook his head. "Not this stuff. Ricky just brought it out of his room this morning after breakfast. We like to have our instruments around at night so we can jam or work out some new tunes."

"This has all gone too far." Woody's face was tight with worry. "First the bike accident, now this." He glanced at Nancy expectantly. "You've got to help us figure this out."

Nancy sympathized with the guys, but she was feeling frustrated by all her unanswered questions. Stepping forward, she said, "I want to help you, but first you have to level with me. I need to know the real story behind all the rumors about the band splitting up."

Woody and Tucker exchanged a guilty look, then Woody nudged the drummer and said, "Okay. Tell her, Tuck."

"All the rumors about us breaking up are just that—rumors," Tucker began slowly. "Our agent thought it would be a good idea to get publicity, but we never thought anyone would get hurt."

"What about the bad feelings toward Courtney?" Nancy prodded.

Woody shrugged. "We've had our share of differences, but they're just growing pains."

"He's right," Tucker agreed. "I'll admit that Courtney isn't my favorite person in the world, but we wouldn't split up over her."

Everything they said made sense. Then why would someone want to hurt Ricky? Nancy glanced uneasily at the musicians as another thought came to her.

"Ricky might not be the only one in trouble," she told Woody and Tucker. "You guys should be careful, too. We don't know who's behind all these accidents. If someone is out to break up the Hot Rods, you guys could all be targets."

"Count me out for the afternoon activities," Nancy told Bess and George as the cousins were putting on their bathing suits after lunch. "I have a few things to take care of."

"But you're going to miss the catamaran cruise," Bess reminded her.

George slipped a T-shirt over her suit and

perched her sunglasses on top of her head. "She can always go on another ride before we leave," George pointed out.

Nancy walked her friends down to the lobby, then went on alone toward the infirmary, a modern building at the opposite end of the resort from the beach. A nurse at the reception area told her that Vincent was still unconscious, and that Ricky was resting quietly. She'd have to wait until later to question Vincent.

Nancy decided it would be a good time to check out Ricky's hotel room. That was where he kept his equipment, and whoever had sabotaged it might have left some sort of clue. She was glad to see that the hallway was empty. Pulling her lock-pick kit from her purse, Nancy opened the door in seconds. She didn't think Ricky would mind, but she didn't want to try to convince the manager that it would be okay.

Glancing about, Nancy let out a loud sigh of disappointment. The hotel maids had already straightened up Ricky's room. Nancy searched carefully but didn't see anything unusual. Lifting the drapes over the sliding glass door that led to a patio, she checked the door for scrapes or dents that would indicate that someone had tampered with the lock. There weren't any, and the door to the hallway also looked clean.

What a waste of time, Nancy thought as she headed back to her own room. Once there, she sat down on the balcony to think, propping her feet up on the railing. If someone had gotten into Ricky's room, it must have been with a key, or else the person knew how to pick a lock. She wondered if it could be a resort employee.

Although she had suspected Vincent of tampering with Ricky's brakes, he couldn't be guilty this time. He'd been sedated since the previous afternoon, and the guys said the cord had been intact then. That meant that possibly another employee was involved—Daniel, or maybe even Gibbs. Gibbs and Ricky had had two arguments that Nancy knew of, and Gibbs would certainly have access to any room in the hotel.

As Nancy tried to put the pieces together, her eyes lit upon the maintenance hut on the cliff. She decided there was no time like the present to check it out. She just hoped most of the staff was busy other places this afternoon.

Nancy made her way quickly down the path to the hut, watching to make sure no one was around. Outside the hut, she placed her ear against the door. When she heard nothing, she tried the door. This time it was locked. Nancy glanced nervously over her shoulder before pulling her small kit from her purse and quickly picking the lock.

Inside, the hut was unchanged. The Polaroid camera was still sitting under a tarp. Flicking on a light, Nancy looked under some of the other tarps. She found a lawn mower and three empty steel barrels—ordinary items for a maintenance hut. She also found a typewriter and another set of file cabinets.

At the far end of the hut was another door, one she hadn't noticed before. I'll check that out as soon as I finish in here, she thought. Going over to one of the file cabinets, Nancy set to work on one of the built-in locks. In the top drawer she found a black ledger book and took it over to the desk, where she opened it under the lamplight.

Each page was dated and contained lists of names with a price beside each one. The figures ranged from ten thousand to thirty thousand dollars. Nancy ran her finger down the names on the list. Her hand stopped abruptly at the third entry under Monday's date. The name was Eva Rivera! Flipping ahead, Nancy found two other names she knew: Eduardo and Juan Cordero!

She closed the book and slipped it back into the drawer, her mind reeling. Money—lots of it—was changing hands. That, combined with the fact that the activity in the hut was conducted after dark, made Nancy pretty sure that whatever was going on had to be illegal. It certainly didn't seem to have anything to do with maintenance!

The question was, *what* was all that money being spent for? Nancy shook her head. Maybe the answer lay in one of the other drawers.

She had just opened another file drawer when she heard a shuffling sound outside. After noiselessly closing the drawer, she searched for a hiding place. She couldn't get caught in there again! She remembered the back door, and opened it.

Pulling the door closed behind her, Nancy felt cool blackness surround her. As her eyes adjusted to the dark, she began to see that she was in some sort of chamber. The walls were rough, as if they'd been carved out of rock. She switched on her penlight and flashed the tiny beam around her. The chamber was a narrow tunnel that cut through the rocks right behind the hut!

With the penlight in one hand, Nancy felt along the rocks with the other as she slowly picked her way through the dark tunnel. She didn't hear anyone behind her, but knew that if the person in the hut had heard her, he might come after her. After a few minutes she saw a dull light just ahead. As she drew closer, she could tell that the light was coming in through the mouth of the tunnel, which was nearly covered by a thick blanket of vegetation.

Nancy pulled aside the mat of flowering vines and stepped out into the bright sunlight. Looking around her, she discovered that she was standing on an oceanside path that zigzagged down along the cliff. With the thick covering of green leaves and red and yellow hibiscus blossoms, no passerby would suspect that a tunnel entrance was hidden in the side of the rocky hill!

Below her the narrow path descended along the edge of the rocks to a small pier. Two boats were tied to the wooden dock. That's it! Nancy thought excitedly. The landing would provide a convenient—and totally camouflaged—way to bring valuables in and out of the resort. Smuggled items? Nancy wondered.

She was making her way down the path toward the boat landing when she heard a noise behind her. Turning, she saw a flash of turquoise and white as a resort employee ducked into the tunnel opening. She didn't have time to retrace her steps to follow him because just then a huge, steel barrel began to roll down the path, directly toward her!

The barrel made a loud clatter, flattening grass and flowers and sending sand and pebbles flying as it picked up speed. Nancy's heart was pounding as she looked from the steep, slick cliff that rose up on her left, to the thin wooden railing on her right—her only protection from a hundred-foot fall to the rocky beach below!

Seeing no place to hide, Nancy took off running down the path. She raced like the wind, but the drum was gaining on her, moving faster every second. Soon it was banging down the path just behind her heels!

Her lungs burning, Nancy realized that the steel barrel was about to flatten her!

Chapter

Twelve

NANCY GLANCED at the wooden railing on her right. It seemed sturdy, but there was no time to test it. She gripped it and jumped over the edge.

Dust and sand flew into her face as the steel drum clattered by just inches from her nose. It kept on rolling, banging, and jumping over ruts in the path. A splinter dug into Nancy's palm as she held on to the rail, her legs dangling in the tropical breeze. Her stomach churned as she glanced down and saw the surf washing over the jagged rocks far below.

Taking a deep breath, she flexed her arms and pulled herself up until she could catch the edge of the path with her leg. Quickly, she rolled onto the path and lay there breathing heavily. Raising her eyes, she looked up at the tunnel entrance, but there was no sign of anyone. Then she hopped up, dusted herself off, and retraced her steps back up the path and to her room, to wait for Bess and George.

"I'm so nervous I can barely eat," Bess said, after Nancy had explained what had happened. When George looked pointedly at her cousin's plate, which was heaped with mango mousse, Bess amended, "Well, almost."

George said to Nancy in a low voice, "I can't believe someone actually tried to kill you!"

Bess waved her fork toward the setting sun, which was casting brilliant colors on the clouds as it sank in the west. "This place may be beautiful, but it seems like Gibbs's 'slice of paradise' is turning into a slice of danger! It's giving me the creeps."

"Obviously, my guess is right," Nancy said. "Some kind of illegal operation is being run out of that hut. Someone wants to stop my investigation before I find out exactly what it is." She jabbed a slice of pineapple and went on. "Well, they're going to find out I don't scare off easily."

"I wish we could set up the stakeout now," George said before taking a bite from a coconut cupcake. "I can't stand the suspense."

Bess glanced nervously across the table. "Me, neither. I want to get this over with."

The cousins had agreed to help Nancy stake out the hut later. "It will be better to wait until

103

later," Nancy told them. "That's when all the activity takes place. Besides, this way we can catch the beginning of Courtney's act in the Coral Cove first."

After dessert they made their way to the new nightclub. The atmosphere of the club was subdued, and three of the walls were lined with glass aquariums lit with cool blue lights. The girls were seated at a table next to a school of bubbling angelfish.

The three girls had just ordered glasses of punch when the lights dimmed on the packed room. From the moment Courtney stepped on stage, her presence lit up the room. Her soulful voice and big brown eyes melted every heart in the audience. Backed by a piano and bass, she did her first set of jazz tunes, and when it ended, everyone cheered.

"She has a great voice," Bess raved, clapping enthusiastically.

Nancy turned as a waitress with frizzy black hair came up to their table. "Are you Nancy Drew?" the girl asked. When Nancy nodded, she said, "Miss Brooks would like to speak with you backstage."

Nancy followed the waitress's directions to Courtney's dressing room and knocked on the door. At the force of her knock, the door swung open all the way.

In the center of the room stood Courtney and

Woody, wrapped in each other's arms, their lips locked in a kiss.

Nancy stood there a moment, wondering if the couple would ever come up for air. Finally she cleared her throat and said, "Uh, I can come back later."

"Oh, no," Courtney answered, turning her flushed face toward Nancy. "I need to talk to you."

Woody blinked. "Nancy," he murmured. "I guess you're the first to discover that Courtney and I have settled our differences."

"We're going to give it another shot." Courtney beamed. "This time, Woody promises he'll learn to trust me. And I'm going to try to keep my nose out of his band's business."

"Try?" Woody echoed, raising an eyebrow.

"Okay, I'll let the Hot Rods make their own decisions." She shot him a sly smile. "You drive a hard bargain."

Nancy grinned at them. "Congratulations!"

"But that's not what Courtney wanted to tell you," Woody added. "She overheard a conversation between Ricky and Steve the other day, and I thought it might be important." He gave Courtney's elbow a gentle squeeze. "Go ahead, tell her."

"Well . . ." Courtney narrowed her eyes as she tried to remember. "It was more like an argument. I was walking on the beach with Steve when Ricky came rushing up to us in a fury. They stepped aside to talk, but I did hear part of their conversation. Gibbs was trying to collect some money from Ricky, but Ricky said he refused to pay until he saw her alive."

Hmm, Gibbs again, Nancy thought. The evidence was piling up against the slick resort owner. But what did it add up to? "Do you have any idea who Ricky was referring to?" she asked. "Could it be his sister Maria?"

The singer shook her head, and Woody spoke up. "We only learned about his sister the other day at lunch, when Ricky went crazy over her earrings."

"What about Gibbs?" Nancy asked Courtney. "Did he say anything to you about their argument?"

Courtney shook her head again. "Sorry. He's always very polite and charming around me. He kind of brushed the argument off, like it was nothing, so I didn't give it another thought."

"Well, thanks for telling me about it," she said, turning to leave. "It's a big help."

Back inside the Coral Cove, Nancy signaled to Bess and George that it was time to leave. The three girls went back to their room to change into dark jeans and cotton sweaters—stakeout clothes, Bess called them.

"I'm still not sure what we're looking for,"

Bess whispered as they moved quietly along the path.

"Neither am I," Nancy admitted. "But I have a funny feeling that the key to the mystery of Pineapple Grove is in that hut."

The girls stopped when they reached a stand of coconut palms. From there they would have to step off the path to reach the hut.

"I don't see any light around the door," Nancy said. "It's probably empty now. George and I will see how we can find out what's going on inside. Bess, you're on lookout."

"Okay," Bess said nervously. "But hurry up— and be careful!"

"This place is sealed up tight," George whispered as she and Nancy circled the hut. "Not even an air vent."

"No windows, either." Nancy paused and stared at the small stucco building. "And since we don't have X-ray vision, we'll have to come up with another approach." She gazed up at the thatched roof. "Feel like doing a little climbing?"

"The roof?" George blinked. "I'm sure we can get up there. But it looks flimsy. Do you think it'll hold us?"

Nancy smiled. "There's one way to find out."

They found a palm tree that arced a few feet away from the rooftop, and Nancy shimmied up it. She held on tight as the tree swayed a little, then gracefully swung down onto the roof.

The straw roof *was* flimsy, but Nancy lay down flat and distributed her weight over a portion of it. It was enough to support her. A moment later George was lying on the roof beside her.

"Now let's see if we can get a look inside." Grabbing a handful of straw, Nancy pulled it loose from the twine sheathing, while George pulled a second clump loose. The rooftop was a few inches thick, but they managed to thin out one spot so that they could see inside.

The hut was empty then, but Nancy and George didn't have to wait long for some activity. As they watched, the lights were switched on.

"There's someone inside," George whispered.

"No one went in through the door," Nancy whispered back, "so he must have come through the tunnel."

Nancy peered through the slit. She was surprised to see a heavyset, jovial resort employee—Daniel! Nancy was willing to bet he was the one who had pushed the steel barrel at her earlier.

With a congenial smile, Daniel led two women in from the tunnel door. He closed the door behind them, pulled the black book from the file cabinet, and logged an entry in it. One woman handed him an envelope. Daniel opened it and pulled out a wad of U.S. dollars.

"Wow!" George mouthed.

"There's the payoff," Nancy whispered. "Now let's see what he sells them."

Daniel motioned for one of the women to sit in front of the screen. Working quickly, he took first her picture, then the other woman's. Nancy watched curiously as he went to a file drawer and pulled out two yellow squares of paper.

"Didn't you suspect Vincent of smuggling jewelry?" George whispered.

Nancy nodded. "But now I think they're dealing in some other illegal trade."

As they whispered, Daniel rolled one of the yellow sheets of paper into the typewriter. It looked like some kind of certificate. Nancy squinted and finally could make out the embossed lettering: Lawful Permanent Resident. Then she noticed the seal of the United States of America.

"Those are U.S. immigration certificates!" Nancy whispered excitedly.

Daniel typed information on both certificates, then escorted the women out the door toward the hotel.

"They take money in exchange for immigration cards," Nancy said in a rush. "They aren't smuggling jewelry—they're smuggling people! The luggage those people were carrying wasn't filled with stolen goods. They were just carrying their personal belongings."

George's mouth dropped open in astonishment. "That means—"

She was interrupted when the door from the

tunnel opened again. This time, Steven Gibbs entered and ushered in what appeared to be a family of three along with their suitcases.

"Gibbs!" George whistled softly.

"Looks like he's in on the operation, too," Nancy whispered. "Or maybe in charge of it."

She was watching Gibbs take a young girl's photo when she heard a stirring noise beside her.

"I'm slipping!" George whispered, grabbing at the roof's thatching.

Nancy reached out to steady her friend, and George managed to grab hold of a bamboo beam. Nancy noticed that the motion had caused a few strands of straw to fall into the hut. She held her breath as they fluttered to the floor just inches from Gibbs's face.

"What's that?" he barked, glaring up at the thatched ceiling.

"We've been discovered!" Nancy whispered as Gibbs jumped up and raced for the door.

Chapter

Thirteen

Nancy glanced down at the ground, but she knew the distance was too great to risk jumping. She and George would have to climb back down the coconut palm tree, and that would take time. Gibbs was sure to see them before they could get away!

"Bess!" Nancy hissed. Bess's head popped up from behind a hibiscus bush. "Gibbs is coming. Stall him."

Bess raced toward the hut, pausing to pick up a coconut. Nancy heard Bess say "Hi" to Gibbs just as he opened the door. "Remember me, Bess Marvin, Mr. Gibbs? Maybe you can help me," she continued.

Gibbs sounded impatient as he asked, "What is it?"

"I was looking for the bunkhouse for male staff. Andrew asked me to meet him there, and I'm late." Bess giggled flirtatiously. "Do you know Andrew? He's one of your lifeguards—the one with the muscles."

Easing herself down the tree trunk, Nancy laughed to herself. Bess was doing a great job! She just hoped Gibbs was falling for it.

Gibbs muttered, "Of course, Andrew . . ."

Nancy jumped the last few feet and scurried into the bushes, with George right behind her.

"Just one more thing," Bess said. "When I was coming down the path, this coconut fell. It hit the roof of your hut, then bounced off and landed at my feet. It almost brained me!" she finished.

Way to go, Bess! Nancy thought. That would explain why pieces of straw had fallen into the room. She held her breath, waiting to see if Gibbs would go for the story.

"It hit the roof?" Nancy heard him ask.

"Almost scared me to death," Bess said. "You should put warning signs under those trees."

Gibbs sounded more relaxed as he told her, "That's not a bad idea, Bess." He gave her directions to the bunkhouse, then disappeared back into the hut.

"What a performance!" George said a minute later as the three girls rushed back down the path.

"Is there really a lifeguard named Andrew?" Nancy asked.

Bess laughed. "Beats me, but Gibbs pretended

that he knew the name. I think he likes to act as if everyone here is part of one big, happy family."

"When the truth of the matter is that Pineapple Grove may just be a cover for a major smuggling operation." Nancy led the girls to a secluded section of the main lobby. The huge, overstuffed basket chairs set in a cozy nook gave them a place to sort out their latest discovery.

"Smuggling?" Bess's eyes widened.

"A people-smuggling operation." Nancy told her what she and George had seen inside the hut. "Gibbs and his men are helping illegal aliens to get out of their native countries. They give their clients U.S. residency cards, then help transport them to the U.S. mainland."

"Though once they have papers, they can fly into the States on their own," George pointed out. "After all, St. John is a U.S. territory. Customs and immigration inspections aren't too strict when you fly in from an American territory."

Nancy nodded. "That's why those guests were coming from the hut at night. The smugglers must bring them in at the secret landing, sneak them through the tunnel, and process their paperwork in the hut. Then the 'guests' can enjoy a few days at the resort before they go off to start a new life in America."

"But why pay to come into the U.S.?" Bess asked, frowning. "Why don't they just come in legally?"

"For some people this is the only way," Nancy explained. "Immigration can be really complicated, and it takes a long time. And if they come from certain countries, where there might be immigration quotas, it's almost an impossibility.

"That explains what Eva was doing here," Nancy continued. "And the Cordero brothers, too. Their names were on the 'client' list in the hut."

"Wow!" Bess exclaimed. "All that money and trouble to sneak into the States. I guess we don't always realize how good we have it."

George was drumming her fingers on the arms of her chair. "But where does Ricky Angeles fit into Gibbs's operation?" she asked.

"Ricky must be trying to smuggle his sister Maria in," Nancy answered.

"Of course!" George whistled through her teeth. "But something must have gone wrong."

Nancy nodded. "That's why he threatened Gibbs."

"Therefore, Gibbs has been trying to have Ricky killed," George added, following Nancy's logic.

"Right. They must have decided it would be easy to eliminate Ricky on the bike trip. Gibbs and Daniel would definitely have access to a master key, so one of them could have slipped into Ricky's room and tampered with his music equipment."

"I guess they didn't count on your brilliant rescues, Nancy," Bess said, grinning.

Nancy thought for a moment. "But something tells me there's more to Ricky's story," she said. "Why would Gibbs try to kill him? He'll never get extortion money with Ricky dead."

Bess shivered. "In other words, this case isn't completely solved yet."

Nancy stood up. "Not until we hear the truth from Ricky Angeles."

"Late-night visitors?" Ricky said, opening the door to his room and motioning for Nancy, Bess, and George to come in. "I just got out of the infirmary tonight."

Ricky turned off his television, then crossed to sit on the edge of his bed. Although he was still pale, he seemed alert and gave them a cheerful smile. "Any news?" he asked.

Nancy told him what they had seen in the hut. "When I discovered that Gibbs was smuggling people in"—she paused before finishing—"I realized that your sister was supposed to be among them."

A look of surprise came over Ricky's face. He stood up abruptly and went to stare out the balcony window. "So you know," he said slowly. "I would have told you, Nancy, but this thing has become dangerous."

"You don't have to convince *us* of that,"

George told him, then described Nancy's narrow escape from the moving steel barrel.

Ricky buried his face in his hands for a moment. "I didn't realize Gibbs was so desperate to keep things quiet. But I should have known. I knew that those close calls weren't accidents."

With a look of resignation, he sat up straight and faced the girls. "Gibbs was supposed to be providing me with an invaluable service," he explained. "For twenty thousand dollars, he promised to get my sister Maria into the States."

"What about you?" Bess asked. "Did you come to the U.S. illegally?"

He shook his head. "Back then the immigration laws were different. When I was a boy, my family was driven out of Mindanao, a southern island of the Philippines, because of the fighting that was going on there. When my parents realized how much danger we were in, they decided to send me to the U.S. with my grandfather."

"What about your parents?" George asked. "Were they reluctant to leave their homeland?"

"They were planning to follow with Maria." Ricky's eyes filled with tears. He swallowed before continuing. "But before the arrangements were completed, they were killed—casualties of the fighting. Maria was all alone. Eight years old and all alone. She stayed with some neighbors, then went to work when she was old enough."

Nancy didn't know what to say. She didn't approve of bringing Maria into the U.S. illegally, but she hoped Ricky could be reunited with his sister. The thought of the young girl left alone was heart-wrenching. Nancy couldn't imagine living through something so terrible.

"What about the immigration authorities?" she suggested after an awkward pause. "Did you try to get Maria in through legal means?"

Ricky nodded wearily. "We've had an application on file at the U.S. Department of Immigration for years. But the processing takes so long. Then once you're approved, there's a quota system. The authorities put a cap on immigrants from certain countries, like Mexico and the Philippines. Right now it's nearly impossible for Filipinos to get into America. Maria would have a chance if she were the wife or daughter of an American citizen. But it takes a lot longer for other relatives, even brothers and sisters. She may never get in legally."

"That must be hard," Bess said gently. "All these years you two have tried to get together, but your countries are keeping you apart."

"It's always been rough on Maria," Ricky admitted. "I was fortunate to have my grandfather in America. But now he's gone, too."

The corners of Ricky's mouth turned down. "It's been an endless struggle. I heard about Gibbs's operation through a friend. I didn't have any trouble talking the band into coming here, and once our agent agreed, everything was set. When I was coming here on the plane, I was so hopeful. I kept picturing Maria's smiling face, knowing that soon she would be in America." His voice became choked with emotion. "But now everything has backfired."

"What happened?" asked George.

"I wish I knew. Gibbs says that she never met his contact on the boat leaving the Philippines, but I don't believe him. I was skeptical when he first explained the delay. Then, when I saw Courtney wearing Maria's earrings, I knew that Gibbs was lying. Those earrings are proof that Maria made it here to Pineapple Grove."

Nancy looked at Ricky. "Where do you think Maria is now?"

Ricky's eyes glimmered with sudden fury. "I'm not sure, but I bet Steven Gibbs knows more than he's letting on."

"Has Gibbs ever tried to increase his fee?" Nancy asked. "Maybe he's keeping her hidden until you come up with more money."

"No." Ricky shook his head. "I still owe him half the money, but he knows I'll pay as soon as I see her, and he's never asked for a penny more than the price we originally agreed on. He just keeps telling me to be patient." He turned to Nancy, a desperate look in his eyes. "I'm afraid something really terrible has happened to her."

As Nancy listened to Ricky, she realized that the situation was much more serious than she had guessed at first. Looking from Ricky to her friends, she said, "This has gone way too far. I think we'd better go to the police."

"No!" Ricky shook his head vehemently. "We can't do that. I won't risk Maria's life."

"Ricky—" Nancy began, but she was interrupted when he pulled a piece of paper from the drawer of the nightstand and handed it to her.

"I found this in my room when I returned from the infirmary," he told her. "Someone must have slipped it under the door."

Nancy stared down at the note typed on plain white paper. There was no signature, but the sender's message was clear: Stay away from the police—if you want to see your sister alive again!

Chapter

Fourteen

THAT'S A pretty strong warning," Nancy commented, passing the note to Bess and George.

Ricky swallowed nervously. "That's why I don't want to get the police involved. Besides, the local police wouldn't listen. Everyone around here adores Gibbs. Pineapple Grove has brought a lot of money and jobs to the area."

"You're right," George agreed. "And it wouldn't be safe to place a call to immigration officials using the resort phone system."

"Still," said Nancy, shaking her head, "we have to find a way to report this." Ricky started to object, but she was emphatic. "Ricky, the immigration agents may be the only ones who can save your sister's life. I can't promise that she'll be admitted to the States, but right now we have to concentrate on finding her—alive."

"And how do you suggest we do that?" Ricky challenged her.

"I'll do my best to track her down." Nancy glanced at her watch. "It's after midnight—a little late to start combing the resort now. But I'll start searching first thing in the morning. Do you have a recent picture of Maria that I can use?"

Ricky pulled his wallet from the back pocket of his jeans and took out a color photograph, which he handed to Nancy.

"Thanks," she told him, studying the smiling face of the pretty, slender girl with dark hair. "This should help."

"What about the police?" George asked.

"Well," Nancy said after a pause, "I think our best bet is to contact the Department of Immigration—personally. So tomorrow morning you and Bess take the early air taxi to Saint Thomas for a tour of the island. First stop, Department of Immigration."

"That's some tour," Bess said jokingly. "I can't wait to hear what you have in mind for the afternoon. But no kidding, Ricky," she added, smiling at the bass player, "we're glad to help out any way we can."

Ricky smiled back at her, but he still seemed nervous. Getting up from the bed, he started pacing again. "What do you want me to do?"

"Stay calm and cool—and be careful," Nancy told him firmly. "We don't want to give Gibbs and his men any more opportunities to hurt you."

Shooting Nancy a worried glance, he asked, "Should I bow out of filming tomorrow? I could help you search the resort."

"No, I don't want you to make any moves that might let Gibbs know we're onto him."

"We'd better go now," Nancy said, heading for the door. "We're going to need a good night's rest!"

The next morning, after seeing Bess and George off at the boat dock, Nancy began a systematic search of Pineapple Grove. She didn't know who on the staff might be involved with Gibbs's operation, so she tried not to attract the attention of anyone wearing a turquoise and white resort uniform. But the staff was so large and helpful that everywhere she turned she ran into a maid asking if she needed directions or a waiter offering her a cool drink!

After three hours of knocking on doors and peeking in windows, she had checked the arts and crafts shop, the bakery, the sports equipment shed, the kitchen, and about a dozen other buildings and sheds. If Maria Angeles was hidden at the resort, Nancy thought dejectedly, her presence was a well-guarded secret.

She decided to check out one last building

before taking a break for lunch. As Nancy approached a long narrow hut just behind the kitchen, she saw steam billowing out from a vent on the roof. She knocked on the door a few times, and when no one answered, she swung the door open and glanced inside to see rows of men and women pressing bed linens with steam machines. A quick look told Nancy that nothing out of the ordinary was going on.

Nancy stepped back on the small porch and closed the door. She turned around—and found herself staring directly into the glaring face of Daniel!

Nancy's heart leaped into her throat. Her face was just inches away from Daniel's brawny neck. His strong hands closed around her arms and moved her aside.

"My, my," he said, laughing. "I've never seen a girl so fascinated with steam pressers before."

How long had he been watching her? she wondered uneasily. Had he just seen her by chance, or had he been keeping an eye on her all morning? Nancy's pulse was racing, but she hid her nervousness with a tight smile.

"Actually, I'm interested in everything that goes on behind the scenes at Pineapple Grove."

"Oh, sure," Daniel teased, but his jovial smile couldn't disguise the cold gleam in his eyes. "All of our guests are fascinated by launderers and bakers."

The bakery was one of the first places she had

checked out that morning. So he *had* been watching her.

"I'm serious. My boyfriend is thinking about opening a hotel, and he asked me to check out everything."

"No fooling? What kind of a boyfriend would ask a pretty girl like you to go snooping around when she could be enjoying herself in the sunshine?" Daniel laughed again, and the hollow sound made Nancy shiver despite the heat.

"I guess I'm just an explorer at heart," Nancy said in a lighthearted tone, ignoring his question.

Daniel gave her a piercing look, then said, "Well, you'd be better off exploring less and relaxing more. That's what Pineapple Grove is all about—a slice of paradise." With a wink, he turned away from her and started down the path.

Nancy watched him until he disappeared from sight, then she turned in the opposite direction and headed toward the terrace for lunch. She still felt uncomfortable, and couldn't help wondering just how much longer she would be safe at Pineapple Grove. Daniel hadn't overtly threatened her, but she knew he was onto her. She had to solve this case, and soon—before something else happened.

Nancy filled her plate with fruit salad, then sat at a table overlooking the beach. As she ate, she turned the clues over in her mind. Unfortunately, she didn't have much to go on when it came to finding Maria Angeles. She had a feeling that she could search the resort for weeks without seeing everything. No, she had to come up with another way of finding Ricky's sister.

As Nancy munched on a slice of coconut, she tried to think of everyone who might know about Maria's whereabouts. Gibbs and his goons knew, of course. But they wouldn't be likely to let such information slip. Unless—

Nancy suddenly stopped chewing as she remembered Vincent Lanchester. He'd been heavily sedated the day before, but maybe his condition had improved. She decided to pay him a visit right after lunch.

"He's talking a little today, but he slips in and out of sleep very easily," the nurse told Nancy at the infirmary.

"May I see him?" Nancy asked. She hoped they didn't have rules limiting visitors.

"Of course."

The nurse directed Nancy to a sunny room with two steel-frame beds. Vincent's eyes were closed, but the patient in the bed beside him was sitting up and reading a magazine. "Hello," the man greeted her. "You here to visit my roomie?"

Nancy nodded. "I need to ask him a few questions—if he wakes up, that is."

"Well, good luck," the man said. "I've been sharing this room for almost a day now, and it seems all he ever does is sleep." He waved his hands in the air and babbled on. "That wouldn't bother me, of course, except that he talks in his sleep. It's very annoying when you're trying to rest."

Without any prompting, the man introduced himself as Melvin Bell, a guest at the resort. He was being treated for sitting on a poisonous sea urchin. "I have red marks all over my— Well, it was painful."

"I'm sure it was," Nancy said politely, then turned to Vincent.

"Can you hear me?" she asked, calling his name.

Vincent stirred, but his eyes remained closed.

When Nancy said his name again, he started muttering. Unfortunately, it was all gibberish. He kept saying something that sounded like "deaf-shane."

"Oh, he's on that kick again," Melvin announced, shaking his head as if he were speaking about a naughty child.

"Pardon me?"

"He says that over and over again. Devil's chain, Devil's chain." Melvin shivered. "Gives me the creeps."

The Devil's Chain? Wasn't that the name of those small islands near the mouth of the cove? Nancy tried to get some kind of response from Vincent, but he merely repeated the same words over and over.

Nancy was frowning as she said goodbye to

Melvin, thanked the nurse, and left the infirmary. She took off her shoes and ambled aimlessly along the beach, deep in thought. Devil's Chain —did it mean anything? As the cool water splashed over her calves, she curled her bare toes in the sand and stared out at the cove.

From there the islands in the Devil's Chain were just tiny black mounds in the water. She stood staring at the bleak-looking islands. Vincent himself had said they were uninhabitable.

That was when it hit her. Had Vincent given away Maria's hiding place? Nancy blinked, then took another look at the black, rocky pieces of land. It was just a hunch, but she had to check it out.

Nancy hurried down the beach to the boathouse, where she arranged to take out a small sailboat. While she was waiting for a staff member to check out the gear, the waterfront director waved Nancy over to him.

"There's a slight hitch with your boat," he said. "We'll have to find you another one. If you'll just wait over there," he said, pointing to the far side of the boathouse, "I'll call you when we get one ready."

As Nancy rounded the corner of the boathouse, she wondered why the director, and not the staff member checking her sailboat, knew the boat wasn't fit to sail. But then she stopped short.

Steven Gibbs was sitting on the edge of a

motorboat, his arms crossed over his chest. "Still exploring, eh, Nancy?" He smiled, but she wasn't fooled by his fake charm.

Nancy glared at him, then realized that it was deserted on this side of the boathouse. A deep sense of foreboding came over her as her eyes darted around the empty dock. But before she could move, everything went black.

Chapter

Fifteen

A DEEP BLUE SKY dotted with silky white clouds whirled above Nancy's eyes. She blinked, wondering why her legs and wrists were throbbing and her head hurt so much. Then she remembered—Gibbs. Someone must have hit her over the head and tied her up.

A sideways glance told her that she was lying in the hull of a motorboat. She heard the rumble of the engine and felt the rocking of the boat as it slapped across the surf.

"Ah, our guest is awake." Gibbs's blond head loomed into view as he leaned over her. "I'm sorry about that little bump on the head, but we didn't want you to miss the cruise, did we?"

An eerie laugh rang out from the rear of the boat, and Nancy recognized Daniel's voice right away. No doubt he was the one who had knocked her out. No one must have seen him hit her, and no one would have noticed her tucked low in the hull as the boat sped out to the cove.

Pushing with her feet, Nancy managed to prop herself up so she could sit upright. Daniel objected at first, but Gibbs called him off.

"We're far enough from shore," he said. "No one will be able to see her. We want our guest to be as comfortable as possible, after all."

Somehow, Nancy didn't think that her comfort was truly his prime consideration. "I should never have listened when that guy asked me to step around the boathouse," she muttered, her head throbbing.

"Who, the waterfront director?" Gibbs asked. "Fortunately, some employees follow directions. He had no idea what we were up to—though, of course, *I* knew what *you* were up to."

He tossed back his blond head in an arrogant gesture and continued, "I was suspicious of that story your friend gave me last night. A bouncing coconut? Come on. When I went back and checked the roof, it was obvious that someone had been spying on us." He leaned closer to Nancy. "In other words, you've been caught snooping around."

Nancy glared at him but didn't say anything.

"Actually," Gibbs continued, "I'm sorry about the turn your whole vacation has taken. Imagine a beautiful girl detective disappearing from an exclusive Caribbean resort! The press will have a field day with us, but I'm afraid I have no other choice."

Looking over her shoulder, Nancy saw that the beach was shrinking from view as the boat moved toward the mouth of the cove. "It won't do you any good to get rid of me," she told Gibbs. "I'm not the only one who knows that Pineapple Grove is just a front for a secret moneymaking operation."

"You make it sound so mercenary," Gibbs protested, "when in fact I'm giving people a chance to buy their freedom. In many cases, I'm reuniting families. I like to see it as a humanitarian endeavor."

"An illegal endeavor," Nancy said.

Gibbs waved off her comment. "Save your arguments for the guys who smuggle drugs and jewels. There's nothing immoral about helping people enter the U.S."

Nancy couldn't believe he really thought that there was nothing immoral about being a criminal! But she had to admit he was a slick one. "How did you come up with copies of the lawful permanent resident certificates?" she asked him. "I thought U.S. documents were difficult to forge —like dollar bills."

"You're right." Gibbs beamed with pride. "But our certificates aren't forged—they're the real thing. I have a good friend in the Department of Immigration who managed to get me a packet of original blank certificates—for a price, of course."

"They're beyond dispute when our clients show them to immigrations officers. We supply our clients with nothing less than the best," Daniel finished with a hearty laugh.

"After we found the means of supplying identification, we only needed to select a convenient location to process our clients' paperwork," Gibbs explained. "I considered a resort on the mainland, but it would have been much more difficult to get our clients past the Coast Guard and border patrol."

Nancy looked at Gibbs curiously. "Doesn't the U.S. Coast Guard patrol the waters in the U.S. Virgin Islands?" she asked.

"Yes, but so far we've been able to give them the slip. It's easier here in the Caribbean, where territorial waters crisscross so much."

"So you built this whole resort as a cover for the smuggling operation," Nancy guessed. Gibbs was turning out to be slimier every second!

"Very perceptive," he told her. "A resort is always filled with people from different countries who are constantly coming and going. What better cover? And most of my clients choose to stay for a few days, as a sort of adjustment period."

He kept on talking, obviously enjoying bragging about his criminal activity. "Once our clients reach the continental U.S., they have the proper paperwork to get a job and a Social Security number. They have all the rights of a citizen. Our system usually works like a charm."

Nancy couldn't believe how arrogant Gibbs was, but at least he was answering some important questions. "What really happened to Eva Rivera? And the Cordero brothers?" she asked.

Gibbs gave Nancy a stern look. "I instructed them to leave immediately after you met them. When your friends told me you were a detective, I kept an eye on you. And it's a good thing, too. In just a matter of an hour or so you almost got that girl Eva's picture as a souvenir. And photographs of my clients could make for damaging evidence."

Nancy nodded. So *that* was why Gibbs had thrown a fit over the appearance of "guests" in the Hot Rods' video. She was beginning to see how all the pieces fit together. Except for one.

Looking closely at Gibbs, she said, "Something went wrong in the case of Maria Angeles. What?"

Gibbs sighed. "I have recently discovered that some of my employees are greedy."

"You call it greed," Daniel chimed in, "Vincent and I call it free enterprise. We take thousands of crisp American dollars into our hands— but they go straight to you. We want a bigger piece of the action."

"I'm not cutting you in, and that's final," Gibbs snapped, losing some of his good humor.

"If you treated us better," Daniel shot back, "we might not have kidnapped the girl."

Nancy watched the exchange between the two men with interest. She had thought that Gibbs had called all the shots—including keeping Maria hostage. Now it seemed that Daniel and Vincent had pulled a fast one behind his back.

"Your feeble attempt at a kidnapping cost me!" Gibbs barked angrily. "How could you be so stupid as to rob the poor girl, then let her die? What kind of ransom do you expect for a dead girl?"

Maria, dead? Nancy didn't want to believe it. She *couldn't* believe it.

"And then the bumbling attempts on Ricky's life—not to mention your little spat with Vincent that landed him in the infirmary." Fury glittered in Steven Gibbs's eyes.

"Vincent was supposed to take care of Ricky Angeles on the bike trip, but he botched it," Daniel said, defending himself. "I didn't mean to hit him that hard, but after he messed up the bike accident, I flew off the handle."

Gibbs turned to Nancy. "Unfortunately, I didn't know anything about all this nonsense until it was too late. Imagine, trying to kill off one of the guests! I only found out about it when Vincent was out of commission and Daniel needed my help in processing our new arrivals." He shot Daniel a reproachful look. "Don't talk to me about more money. Incompetence will not be rewarded. Your foolishness has put our entire operation at risk."

Nancy noticed that they were approaching the Devil's Chain. Now that Maria was dead, the rocky, blackened clumps of land looked more threatening than ever. Gibbs and Daniel had answered all her questions about the case, but now they were going to make sure she kept quiet about it—for good!

Nancy was still looking at the Devil's Chain when Gibbs turned back to her. "I really am sorry that things have to end this way. Killing people is not what Pineapple Grove is about," he said with a sigh. "But now that Daniel and Vincent started this mess, I have to see it through to protect my interests."

Daniel cut the engine as the boat reached one of the rocky islands, and used an oar to navigate carefully through the jutting rocks. Finally he grabbed a craggy boulder and anchored the boat to it.

Gibbs stood up and climbed from the boat to the boulder. "Shall we?"

Before Nancy knew what was happening, Daniel lifted her in his arms and draped her over his shoulder. As she was being carried, Nancy searched frantically for a means of escape. She saw none—her only hope was in trying to talk some sense into Gibbs.

"You'll never get away with this," she called, bouncing against Daniel's back.

"Save your breath," Gibbs said.

A moment later Nancy felt herself being lowered to the ground. Daniel grabbed her by the waist and dragged her into a sitting position on the sandy bottom of a tide pool. Nancy gasped as seawater seeped into her sneakers and clothes. The water level came up to her shoulders, and she was leaning against the smooth edge of a large rock. "What are you trying to do?" she asked.

"Destroy incriminating evidence," Daniel said as he looped a rope around Nancy's waist and tied her to the boulder. "At the moment, that includes you. You got away from that steel barrel. But this time the ocean will do our dirty work for us."

It was no use arguing with him. After all, he'd already tried to kill both her and Ricky. Nancy looked around at Gibbs. "Steven, you can't condone this. It's just not your style," she said in as firm a voice as she could.

Gibbs merely shrugged, then glanced at his watch. "Our timing is just right. The tide is coming in." As he spoke, a wave crashed over the surrounding rocks, spraying salt water into Nancy's face.

Nancy blinked until the stinging sensation was gone from her eyes. If the tide was coming in, the water level in the tide pool would be rising. In just a few minutes it would be over her head!

Daniel smiled down at her. "I'll be back in a

few hours to cut off the ropes." His hollow laughter chilled her.

"The coroner's report will say death by drowning," Gibbs said wistfully. "And everyone will mourn the foolish girl who swam too far from shore."

Drowning! Nancy squirmed, but the rope around her waist kept her in place.

"Don't add murder to the charges you're already facing," Nancy told Gibbs. "Juries don't take kindly to killers."

"There will be no charges at all," Gibbs said calmly. "Why do you think I'm going to the trouble of eliminating you?"

In a much calmer voice than she felt, Nancy said, "My friends went to the authorities this morning. Immigration agents and local police are probably waiting for you at the resort this very minute!"

"Ah, yes, George Fayne and Bess Marvin. My people told me they were taking the air taxi to Saint Thomas this morning." Gibbs shook his head. "I had a hunch that they were part of your little detective team. That's why I took the precaution of calling an old acquaintance of mine, in Saint Thomas. He's very good with a knife. Of course," Gibbs continued, "my friend will make it look like a robbery. Two unfortunate tourists who resisted a mugger and paid the price with their lives."

Nancy shivered as she listened to Gibbs's

chilling words. A helpless feeling wrenched at her.

"I haven't yet decided what to do with Ricky Angeles." Gibbs tapped his chin thoughtfully, as if he were considering what color wallpaper to use in the resort lobby. "I may try to buy his silence, since he's incriminated himself by trying to buy his sister's freedom. On the other hand, it might be best just to dispense with him, too. I hate loose ends, don't you?"

Nancy gasped. "Come on, Gibbs," she called out in desperation. "You're not a killer! Call this thing off before it's too late."

"No. I'm a businessman, and I'll do whatever it takes to protect my interests."

Daniel tugged on the rope one more time, then the two men stepped back.

"Goodbye, Nancy," Gibbs said politely. "It's been a pleasure. But soon it will be high tide— and then farewell to Nancy Drew."

Chapter

Sixteen

GIBBS AND DANIEL turned and climbed over the jagged rocks and out of sight. A few minutes later Nancy heard the motorboat roar to life, then the sound fade as it sped away.

She glanced down at the rising water, which now reached halfway up her chest. She had to get out of the tide pool before it was too late!

Nancy pushed against the sandy bottom, but the rope around her waist was just tight enough to keep her down. If she could loosen the bindings on her hands and feet, she thought desperately, she'd have a chance of escaping.

A giant wave crashed over the rocks, and Nancy sputtered as water hit her face. When her vision cleared, she searched the bottom of the tide pool. The rope on her ankles seemed to be a little worn. She knew she couldn't break it, but a sharp object might cut through it.

Nancy felt around quickly with her hands, but the surface of the boulder was as smooth as glass. As she felt to the right, however, she found that the rock jutted out into a shelf.

"Ouch!" she said, wincing as she reached under the rock shelf. Small, sharp objects were growing there. Barnacles!

The water had already reached Nancy's shoulders. Working quickly, she stretched her wrists apart until the rope between them was taut, then she rubbed the rope against the sharp, calcified shells. After a few minutes she stopped rubbing to feel the rope with her fingers. It was shredding but too slowly. The water was up to her chin!

Panic welled up inside Nancy as she worked the bindings against the barnacles. Her heart raced with each wave that splashed into the deepening tide pool. She gave the rope another pull and—snap! It split in two. Her hands were free!

Nancy flexed her fingers, then quickly went to work on the double knot around her waist. The tide had risen so high that she now had to strain upward, take deep breaths, and work underwater.

Finally the knot loosened and Nancy ripped it open. The slackened rope floated away from her as she propelled herself above the surface, gasping for air.

She was free!

Taking huge, gulping breaths, Nancy crawled back onto the boulder and reached down to untie the rope around her ankles. There wasn't a minute to spare. She had to find a way back to St. John to stop Gibbs and his men from killing her friends—if it wasn't too late already!

Finding small toeholds, Nancy slowly scaled the jagged cliffside. As she climbed, she tried to remember everything Vincent had told them about the Devil's Chain that day in the glass-bottomed boat. Hadn't he said something about dark pits you could fall into? she thought nervously.

She kept away from the shadows, pausing when she reached a wide stone ledge. From there she could cut inland, away from the barren cliffs, and search the island for trees and plants. If she could find some dry brush, she could start a signal fire to attract the attention of passing boats and planes.

She was crossing the ledge when she noticed a dark opening in the rock. Edging closer, she saw that it was the mouth of a cave. Her skin prickled as she peered into the blackness.

Nancy froze as she glimpsed a movement in the cave. She blinked, trying to adjust her eyes to the darkness. Soon she was able to make out a shadowy figure. Her pulse pounded in her ears as she tried to focus in the darkness. She couldn't tell what the creature was, but it was moving toward her!

Nancy backed out of the cave and flattened herself against the stone wall, gripping the jagged surface. She gasped as the figure stepped out onto the sunny ledge.

It was a young woman! She was barefoot and her clothes were tattered, but she moved with a graceful stride. The slight, dark-haired woman glared suspiciously at Nancy.

As Nancy got a closer look at the girl's almond-shaped brown eyes and pale complexion, she knew immediately who she was—she had stumbled onto Ricky Angeles's sister!

"Maria?"

A puzzled expression crossed the girl's face. "How do you— You're not with them, are you?" she asked, backing away.

"Your brother sent me to find you," Nancy explained gently, trying to calm the girl down. "Ricky's been worried sick about you." She smiled warmly at Maria. "I'm Nancy Drew, a friend of your brother's. Are you okay?"

Maria was baffled as she shook Nancy's hand. "I'm fine. How did you find me here?"

"That's a long story," Nancy said. "I'll try to explain everything as we work, but first we need to start a signal fire. Do you know where we can find some dry leaves or grass?"

"Follow me," Maria said with a nod. As she led Nancy from the stone ledge to a sandy path, she explained. "I've combed every inch of this island in the days that I've been here. I was left here by two men, who stole all my things then went off in a motorboat. After my long trip from the Philippines, I was so exhausted I didn't know what to do."

"It must have been terrifying," Nancy said sympathetically.

"The first day I just cried. I hoped and prayed that the men would come back for me." She paused as she pointed out a half-hidden pit that they had to step around.

"Then I decided I had to survive. So I started exploring the island. I found fish to eat and wove a mat to sleep on. When the two men came back on the third day, I hid from them." Maria laughed. "Boy, were they mad! I watched them from my cave, stumbling about and screaming at each other."

Nancy chuckled to herself, imagining the scene. They must have been embarrassed at losing their hostage! No wonder they had told Gibbs that Maria was dead. "They were trying to use you to get money from your brother," Nancy told Ricky's sister.

Maria nodded. "I thought of that, and that was one of the reasons I hid from them. They came back to search for me a few more times, but I decided to take my chances alone on the island rather than trust them again."

"You're very brave," Nancy said as they rounded a rocky cliff that gave way to a flat, grassy clearing edged with palm trees.

Together they made quick work of lighting a signal fire. While Maria gathered dry leaves, Nancy reached into the pocket of her shorts. Her lock-picking kit was there, a little soggy, but intact. She opened it up and pulled out a small magnifying glass.

They stacked the dry brush, then Nancy held the glass in front of a leaf. When the sun shone through the glass, a brown spot formed on the leaf and it began smoking. A moment later a flame popped up, and the brush picked up the flame. The fire grew in size.

Nancy watched as black smoke billowed into the air. "Someone is bound to notice this. But let's write a message, in case someone is flying overhead. They might think this is just a brush fire."

Maria helped her gather smooth black stones, which they arranged in the center of the field, spelling out the letters SOS. When they were finished, each letter was about four feet long and two feet wide.

They had barely finished when they heard the whir of a helicopter. Running to the middle of the message, they searched the sky until finally the red-and-white chopper came into view.

"The U.S. Coast Guard!" Nancy exclaimed. "That was fast!"

The helicopter circled once, then slowly dropped straight down into the field a few feet from their stones. Nancy was so relieved, she wanted to kiss the pilot. She settled for a friendly handshake after she and Maria climbed aboard the craft.

"Welcome aboard, ladies," the pilot said. "I have to admit, I only expected to find one young woman on the island, but I consider this a bonus. Is one of you Maria Angeles?"

"That's me."

"You're the one I'm looking for. I just got word on the radio that you were stranded somewhere in the Devil's Chain. Your signal fire helped me find you right away." He turned back to the control panel and took the copter back into the air.

Nancy leaned forward. After introducing herself, she asked, "Can you radio ahead to the police on Saint Thomas? I have reason to believe that my friends are in grave danger there."

"Bess Marvin and George Fayne?" he repeated after she gave him the names. "They're the girls who sent us the message from Pineapple Grove. Seems they've caused quite a stir there. The place is swarming with police and immigration agents."

"They made it back!" Nancy shouted, relief flooding through her. "Then they're okay?"

The pilot shrugged. "They were in good enough shape to turn Steven Gibbs's resort upside down."

"All right!" Nancy cried.

Ten minutes later the helicopter set down on Pineapple Grove's landing pad.

"Ricky!" Maria Angeles hopped out of the helicopter and ran across the pavement, straight into her brother's arms.

Nancy's heart went out to them as she watched the tearful reunion. They both had suffered through so much to be together. She hoped they could work something out with the immigration authorities so that Maria could stay in America.

Stepping down to the ground, Nancy crossed over to where Bess and George were standing with the other two Hot Rods. Bess and George looked completely surprised to see her.

"Nancy!" Bess exclaimed. "What were you doing in the Devil's Chain?"

When Nancy explained how she had been taken to the island where Maria was hiding, Bess became furious. "Gibbs and Daniel were arrested just a few minutes ago, and they didn't say a word about leaving you out there to die. What creeps!"

Nancy grinned at Bess, relieved that they were all together—and all alive and well. "How did you know Maria was there?" Nancy asked. "Did Gibbs and Daniel tell you that much, at least?"

"No," George answered. "That information

came from Vincent after he regained consciousness. It seems he had a change of heart after his accident. He confessed to the nurse in the infirmary, and she reported everything to the local police. Unfortunately, no one could make sense of the story until we came back with the authorities from Saint Thomas."

Bess gestured to someone behind Nancy, and Nancy turned to see a short, squat man walking over to her. He stepped forward and shook Nancy's hand, introducing himself as Special Agent Lowery. "You've uncovered quite a network of illegal activity here. Nice work."

"Thanks for flying in with my friends." Nancy smiled. Turning back to George and Bess, she told them Gibbs's story about the hired killer who was supposed to greet them in Saint Thomas. "I was worried sick about you guys!"

Bess and George exchanged a look of astonishment, then burst into laughter.

"What's so funny?"

"Do you think—" Bess began.

"It had to be." George nodded at her cousin, then explained to Nancy, "When we got off the plane, two other women on the flight were walking in front of us on the pier. Some guy jumped out and pulled a knife on them. I thought he was robbing them!"

"George knocked the knife out of his hand with a kick," Bess said. "Then I pushed him in the water," she finished proudly.

George shrugged. "He must have been told to look for two young women. He just picked the wrong ones."

"We had the advantage because we caught him off guard," Bess added. "He didn't expect two bystanders to get involved."

George laughed again. "We didn't connect it to the case. I just assumed he was a thief."

Nancy gave them each a hug. "Thank goodness you were both on your toes."

"I guess some of your detective's instincts have rubbed off on us," Bess said with a smile.

"We've learned from the best," George added.

"Bring on Woody and the Hot Rods!" Bess cheered.

It was later that day, and Pineapple Grove's dance club was loud with excitement. Nancy, George, and Bess were sharing a table with Courtney.

"It's great of the Hot Rods to give a special show," said George, sipping a banana milkshake.

"They wanted to prove once and for all that they're together." Dressed in an emerald green minidress, Courtney looked beautiful and happier than ever.

Glancing down at the diamond engagement ring Courtney wore, Nancy asked, "When are you and Woody getting married?"

Courtney shrugged. "We're not sure yet. Sometime between tours. And we're determined to make it work."

"Mind if I join you?"

The girls looked up to find Maria arm in arm with her brother.

"We'd love it," Bess said, pulling out a chair for her.

Ricky waved, saying, "Got to run, you guys. See you after the show."

Maria turned to Nancy with a bright smile. "Good news! I've been given a visa so that I can stay in the U.S. until my paperwork is processed."

"That's great!" Nancy told her.

"The immigration authorities say that my case is an exception. Since my parents were killed in a political struggle, I'll be granted political asylum."

Everyone at the table congratulated Maria and wished her the best. They were still talking about her move to America when the lights dimmed and the Hot Rods appeared on stage.

Their first song had the audience clapping and singing along. Woody called for a few volunteers from the audience, and Courtney and Bess ran up to the stage, along with a handful of female fans.

George nudged Nancy and nodded toward the stage. "Is that Bess singing off-key?"

Nancy listened closely, then shook her head.

"No. In fact, I think she's bucking for a record contract of her own."

Bess had actually grabbed one of the microphones. "Hold on, baby . . ." she crooned in a sultry voice.

George smiled. "That's our Bess!"

Nancy's next case:

Nancy's worried about her boyfriend, Ned Nickerson. He can't take his mind off his job as an investigator for an insurance company. Convinced that a man named Toby Foyle has filed a false injury claim, Ned seems prepared to go to any length to prove his case.

Nancy decides the only way to help is to join the investigation. But a late-night phone call gives her an even more chilling cause for concern. The Toby Foyle case has taken an ugly turn: Foyle has turned up dead—and Ned's fingerprints have turned up on the murder weapon . . . in *HIGH RISK*, Case #59 in The Nancy Drew Files™.

SUPER HIGH TECH . . .
SUPER HIGH SPEED . . .
SUPER HIGH STAKES!

He's daring, he's resourceful, he's cool under fire. He's Tom Swift, the brilliant teen inventor racing toward the cutting edge of high-tech adventure. But Tom's latest invention—a high-flying, gravity-defying, superconductive skyboard—has fallen into the wrong hands. It has landed in the lair of the Black Dragon.

The Dragon, also known as Xavier Mace, is an elusive evil genius who means to turn Tom's toy into a weapon of world conquest! Swift will have to summon all his skill and cunning to thwart the madman. But the Black Dragon has devised a seemingly impenetrable defense system: he appears only as a laser-zapping hologram!

Turn the page for your very special preview of the first book in an exciting new series . . .

THE BLACK DRAGON

Don't tell me I look like a geek," Tom Swift warned his friend Rick Cantwell. But he was grinning as he spoke into the microphone built into his crash helmet.

Tom knew he looked—well, weird. Besides the helmet that covered his blond hair, he was wearing heavy pads at his knees, elbows, and shoulders to protect his lean form. But weirdest of all were the heavy straps that bound his feet to an oversize surfboard, miles from any beach.

"I wouldn't say geek." Rick Cantwell's chuckle came clearly through Tom's earphones. "I'd say ner-r-r—"

His voice went into a stutter as Tom twisted a dial on the control panel at his waist. The surfboard under Tom's feet started humming loudly, then floated three feet off the ground.

Rick ran a hand through his sandy

brown hair, finally getting his voice back. "This is— I can't even say. It's like magic!"

"Not magic—electricity," Tom said, laughing. "Let's try it out."

He twisted a dial on the control panel. The humming grew louder, and the board sped up, skimming over the putty brown track on the ground. The track—a specially designed electromagnetic carpet— was just as important as the board. When the carpet powered up, it produced a giant electromagnetic field that "pushed" against the superconductive material in the skyboard, making it float.

"Okay, now," Tom said, turning up the dial. "Let's see how it moves."

The board picked up speed, riding on an invisible wave of magnetism. Tom bent forward a little, like a surfer playing a wave.

"It's like something out of a comic book. Look at that sucker go!" Rick yelled as Tom flashed past. "How fast can you push it?"

Tom shook his head.

"The problem with you, Rick, is you've got a reckless streak," Tom told him. "For you, there's only one setting worth trying— maximum. That's why *I'm* testing this board instead of you. You're a walking definition of the engineering term 'test to destruction.' "

"Yeah, but how fast does it go?" Rick asked.

Tom sighed. "*You'll* have to tell *me*. There's a radar gun—"

"Got it!" Rick said. "I'll just aim as you pass by and—" Rick's voice cut off with a loud gulp. "Um, would you believe seventy-five?"

Tom was crouched on the board now, looking as though he were fighting a strong wind—and he was. Air resistance of more than seventy miles an hour was trying to tug him off the board.

"This is serious," Rick said. "When do I get my turn?"

"Serious?" Tom started to laugh. "It sure is ... so why am I having such a good time?"

"Hey, don't let your dad know." Rick was laughing, too.

"No, we'll just give him the facts and figures," Tom said. "Like how this thing climbs."

Using the left-hand dial to throttle back the speed, Tom turned the right-hand dial. "Yeeaaah!" he yelled as the board went screaming into the sky.

"Tom!" Rick shouted. "Are you okay?"

"Yeah." Tom's voice was a little shaky as he answered. "Make a note for Dad. This thing climbs like a jet plane."

The skyboard was making a lazy circle about a hundred feet in the air. Tom stared down. If he were a little higher, he could probably see Los Angeles. As it was, all of Central Hills was laid out at his feet.

Right below him, half-hidden in the hills, were the four square miles of Swift Enterprises. Tom could see the landing strips for planes and helicopters and the rocket launch site, but the center of his orbit was the testing field.

Tom noticed that the area was filling up with people. The technicians at Swift Enterprises were used to seeing strange things, but an eighteen-year-old on a surfboard with ten stories of thin air under him—that got attention.

Tom quickly brought the skyboard down to the ground, kicked free of the straps, and went over to Rick. "Let's set up the maneuverability test." He bent over the operations console, flicked a switch, and spoke into the microphone. "Robot! Do you hear me?"

"Receiving loud and clear." The robot sat in the center of the oval track, at a console that was a twin to the one Tom used. Around the robot a pattern of hatches was spread on the ground, making it look like a giant checkerboard.

"What are you supposed to be doing?" Rick's broad, good-natured face looked puzzled. "Playing chess?"

"Each square out there is a separate cell with a small but powerful electromagnet." Tom reached over to one side of the board and flicked some switches. "The trapdoors hide different, um, obstacles."

"What kind?" Rick asked.

Tom grinned. "Watch and see."

He hopped back on the skyboard, brought it to humming life, and took off. This time, instead of going around the test track, he swept across it onto the checkerboard. "When I reach you, robot, the test is over."

"Understood." The robot's hands flew across the control console.

Instantly, a hatch on the ground opened, and blasts of compressed air tried to blow Tom off the board. Tom sent the board into a zigzag, avoiding the blasts.

"Some test, Swift," Rick needled Tom over his headphones. "It looks more like a giant fun house."

A hatch directly in front of Tom opened, and a jet of water burst out of a huge squirt gun. Grabbing the control knobs at his waist, Tom sent the board hurtling out of the line of fire.

Hatches were opening up all around the checkerboard, sending a wild assortment of "weapons" at Tom. Bags of flour, squirts of paint, and even a barrage of cream pies went into the air. But Tom wove through the pattern of "fire" without being touched, like a hotdogger on an invisible wave.

"You're almost there," Rick said excitedly.

Tom brought the board around for a landing behind the control console. The robot swiveled its head, its photocell eyes gleaming. Then its hand shot out to the power-grid controls, twisting a dial.

"Hey! You're not programmed to—"

That was as far as Tom got as the electromagnetic grid below him went crazy. The board bucked under his feet like an animal trying to toss him off.

Then it swooped into the air on a wild course, completely out of control. Tom struggled desperately, using the dials on his waist panel to try to straighten the skyboard.

He'd almost succeeded when a random magnetic blast first jerked the board, then sent it tumbling. Tom's feet were knocked right out of the foot straps.

Then he was falling, with nothing below him but seventy feet of thin air—and the hard, cold ground.

Tom threw out his arms like a skydiver, trying to slow his fall. "Rick—the air bags!" he yelled into his helmet mike.

Big white patches blossomed on the ground as Rick triggered the air bags. Then Tom's whole world turned white as he crashed into a mountain of inflated cushions.

That evening, at the beach, Tom unwrapped two skyboards—one red, one blue. Rick laid out the control panels and helmets and pads.

"You think of everything, Swift," he said, "even racing jackets." He held one up. "But couldn't you come up with something a little more stylish? Like black leather? This is kind of bulky, and it comes down below my hips."

"It's for safety, not fashion," Tom said. "There's a little ring up by the neck piece. If you get into any trouble on the board, yank it."

"And?" Rick said.

"And a dynasail comes out," Tom told him. "It fills with compressed air in about three seconds and is totally maneuverable. Rob put it together, based on some doodles I did."

Rick shook his head. "Let's hope we don't have to test *that*."

A crowd of kids came from the bonfires to marvel at the glowing track. Tom's sister, Sandra, came, too, carrying a plate heaped with hamburgers. "Some supplies for your trip," she said, a grin on her pretty face.

"Mmm, delicious." Rick grabbed another burger and started eating.

"How about you, Tom?" Mandy Coster asked.

"I'll have just one." Tom glanced at Rick. "Got to keep my racing weight down." He grinned as Rick nearly choked.

Pulling a cable he'd run from the van he used as a mobile lab, Tom hooked it up to the superconductor track he had sprayed on the sand. "We'll let it charge up while we get into our gear."

Rick slipped into the padding and jacket but stared at the helmet. "I can understand the mike and earphones, but I wouldn't think you'd need a tinted visor for night flying."

Tom grinned as he pulled on his own equipment. "Try it."

Rick put the helmet on. "I still don't see—" he began, slipping the visor down. "But I do now!"

Tom pulled down his visor—and the darkness around him disappeared. He could see everything clearly, but it looked like the landscape of another planet. The beach and the hills beyond were all tinted red, and the people around him glowed slightly. A brilliant band of color tinged the sky in the west, where the sun had set. The flame of the bonfire was blinding.

"Night vision!" Rick exclaimed.

"Ruby-lensed infrared visors," Tom said. "They actually read heat waves—the warmer the object, the brighter the light."

"Great. Well, I'm ready to go." Rick grabbed a board and headed for the track.

"This spray-on film isn't as strong as the other track," Tom warned. "We'll probably go up only a couple of feet—if we go up at all."

"Just one way to find out," Rick said, clamping his feet into the foot straps.

Tom tested the radio link with Rick and with his sister, who stood at the mobile lab's control board. "Sandra," he said into his mike, "everything ready?"

"Looks good from here," she said. "I'll move in with remote control if anything goes wrong."

"Okay, then." Tom clamped on his own straps. "Let's go for it!"

He and Rick moved the height controls. The boards floated into the air, bringing gasps from the kids. Tom could hear someone yell, "Outrageous!"

"How's it feel?" Tom asked Rick.

"A little wobbly," his friend replied.

"The spray must be a little uneven, so the magnetic field is uneven, too." Tom didn't mind the feeling. He felt as if he were bobbing on water. "Let's try once around the track," he said, "just to get the hang of it."

"Okay," Rick responded. "Then, when we come past Sandra, we'll speed it up."

His hand went to the speed control, and Tom followed. Their movement was more choppy than smooth, but they could handle it. Increasing the speed helped.

As they passed Sandra, Rick really poured it on. He whipped ahead of Tom, who sped up to pull even with him again.

"How about a little race?" Rick asked. Tom couldn't see Rick's face through the visor, but he knew his friend was grinning a challenge at him.

"Okay. But keep it under seventy—hey!"

Rick shot off again, with Tom zooming in pursuit. The slight roughness of the ride made the race more exciting. Instead of floating easily, Tom felt as if he were on the crest of a monster wave of energy, always on the brink of falling. The wind pulled at him as he upped his speed again.

Five feet ahead, Rick bent to cut his air resistance. Tom crouched a little lower, cutting his own wind profile. The clump of spectators passed in a blur.

"Hey, guys . . ." Sandra's voice cut in over their earphones. "We just clocked you doing ninety!"

Tom moved to slow down, but Rick just whooped and sped up. Then they were suddenly swooping up, gaining altitude at an incredible rate. "What the—?" Tom yelled, fighting his controls.

"You're not responding to remote control." Sandra's voice sounded scared.

"Tom—we've left the track!" Rick yelled. They still swept on, controlled by another magnetic field.

"Time to bail out," Tom said, tearing loose from the foot straps. He grabbed the ring on his jacket, pulled, and felt the dynasail fill and expand. He maneuvered it easily down to the beach.

But when he looked for Rick's dynasail, Tom saw him still crouched over his board. "Forget about it," Tom said. "Get off now!"

"I—I can't!" Rick's voice was tight. "My foot strap is stuck."

A tight, cold fist squeezed Tom's stomach as he watched his friend leave the magnetic field and start tumbling to the ground. "Rick!" he yelled.

A black shape came whispering out of

the sky. Through his infrared visor, Tom recognized the shape of an attack helicopter, painted and modified for a stealth mission.

The chopper dropped like a striking hawk for Rick and his board, a net flying out to catch them in midair.

As Tom stared, the dark intruder changed course, heading up and east while it drew his netted friend inside.

Inside the Black Dragon's complex, Tom saw swarms of worker robots turn, form ranks, and march off together. It was as if a single mind controlled them. Tom shivered. A single mind *did* control them—Xavier Mace. The disturbing question was, what did he intend to do with them?

Then, ahead of him and Rob—his seven-foot robot—he saw the small lab building that was their target.

Rob, back on the sensors, reported, "The entire place is surrounded by a high-energy electron field. And there are faint traces of a human presence inside the walls."

"Rick!" Tom said. "Well, the longer we wait, the more time we give the Black Dragon to get something unpleasant ready. Come on, Rob. We're going in."

In a moment, Tom stood outside the lab building, his duffel bag in hand and Rob by his side.

"Nothing's happening," Tom said as they walked toward the door. He pulled a little white disk out of his bag and stuffed it down the data slot. The locking mechanism went crazy, and the door slid half open.

A white-faced Rick Cantwell stood in the center of the room. His fists were clenched, and an ugly bruise stretched from his cheek to the line of his jaw. "I'm ready for you this time—"

His words cut off as he recognized the robot in the doorway. "Rob?" he said, the word mingling disbelief and delight. "Where's—?"

Tom lifted the visor on his helmet.

Rick's shoulders slumped in relief. "About time you came to get me." He started to grin, but it obviously hurt his face. "How'd you get in here without getting burned to a crisp? There's about ninety million volts of electricity outside."

"I don't have to worry about that in this suit," Tom said. "But you will." He reached into his bag of tricks. "We'll just have to—"

The huge screen on the wall flashed to life, revealing the face of the Black Dragon.

"Do I have the pleasure of talking to Tom Swift?" he asked.

"You do," Tom told him. "Though I don't know why it should please you."

"It's always a pleasure to talk to someone who invents an elegant solution to a difficult problem," Xavier Mace said with a smile. "In reverse engineering the samples of your skyboard that I obtained, I came to a lively appreciation of your genius. That's why I'm giving you this warning."

The face on the viewscreen leaned forward a little. "The secret of your superconductor is no longer a secret. Using the new technology, my automated work force is already producing a selection of attack robots."

Mace's smile became wider. "You have one minute to surrender, Tom Swift."